Metta Victoria Fuller Victor

Uncle Ezekiel

And His Exploits On Two Continents

Metta Victoria Fuller Victor

Uncle Ezekiel
And His Exploits On Two Continents

ISBN/EAN: 9783743423886

Manufactured in Europe, USA, Canada, Australia, Japa

Cover: Foto ©Andreas Hilbeck / pixelio.de

Manufactured and distributed by brebook publishing software
(www.brebook.com)

Metta Victoria Fuller Victor

Uncle Ezekiel

UNCLE EZEKIEL;

AND

HIS EXPLOITS ON TWO CONTINENTS.

BY

MRS. METTA V VICTOR.

LONDON:

GEORGE ROUTLEDGE AND SONS,

THE BROADWAY, LUDGATE.

UNCLE EZEKIEL'S EXPLOITS.

CHAPTER I

PETER POTTER'S CABIN.

THE squatter, Peter Potter, sat in the door of his cabin watching the sun go down, far away over the prairie. His hard, browned face glowed red in the crimson light.

"Dry, dry!" he muttered. "It'll be as dry as an unmilked cow, by the sign of the sun's going down so hot and red. I deelar', this is bad." And he looked with anxiety toward the field of stunted corn which lay at the right of the house. He had reason to feel troubled, for not a drop of rain had fallen for three weeks; and the whole dependence of his family for food during the ensuing year would be in the corn-crop and potatoes. If the corn should be searce, they would not have the wherewithal to fatten the two pigs grunting lazily in a sty a little back of the eabin; children and pigs would suffer together.

There was no market within a hundred miles of the squatter, and but few neighbors within that distance. He had settled in this remote spot beeause the prairie-land was rich and easily tilled, requiring no wearisome proeess of elearing, and he could help himself to as much as he desired. His tent was pitehed, that is to say, his shanty was erected, with rare discrimination for a squatter, in the midst of a clump of trees on a slight rise of ground, about a rod from a large spring whose waters flowed from the hill-side and ran over in a triekling· stream which served to irrigate his land. Yet 'ven this supply was not enough to keep his cornfield from turning yellow, and, for the last two or three days, he saw that the spring itself had fallen considerably If its supplies should give out, through the failure of its sources, he knew that great suffering would be the consequence; therefore he had been watching the indications of the heavens with earnestness, and was not a little troubled to see the sun sink like a ball of red-hot iron heavily below the horizon.

"I declar', wife," he said, looking back into his cabin, "thar's no more prospect of rain, till the moon changes, if then. The sun's gone down as red as the kiver of that bake-kittle you're licatin' on the coals thar'. The corn's wiltin' down like a girl that's sick with the heart-distemper—here it is nigh unto the middle of July, and the tallest of it ain't as high as our two-year-old."

"Well, the Lord have mussy on us, if the spring gives out, we'll have to take the young ones on our backs, and start for a new place," she replied, in the patient tone of a woman who has lived two years in a new country, and become accustomed to all manner of disasters.

"No great danger of that, I hope, Melissy," answered the squatter sturdily.

He was an energetic man, whose will arose in proportion to the difficulties to be encountered; he was already beginning to recover from the slight feeling of depression occasioned by the unusual weather. His wife, who had great respect for his abilities, and trusted meekly in his judgment, brightened up, at his cheerful tone, setting her dishes on the table with the quick steps of health and content.

"I wonder where in 'arth them children be," she continued presently. "I hain't seen 'em for two hours, and supper's most ready. I expect, every day of my life, they'll git lost or snake-bitten, or suthin' arnother. Oh, yer there, Dan, Amos!" she called, going to the door, and leaning out over her husband's shoulder. Two curly-headed, brown-faced boys of six and seven years of age, appeared around the corner of the unfenced cornfield, in answer to her summons. "You're thar', be you?"—and she went back to her work.

"I wish you'd come here, Melissy, and see if you can make out who that is, comin' over from the direction of our new neighbor's." Said Peter, a few moments later.

She just stopped to put the cover on the bake-kettle, so that the johnny-cake might be doin' before she came and looked out. "'Pears to me it's that same person as came here last week to borrow the ax and flat-irons. I can make him out quite plain now. I ought to have gone over, and seen if they wanted any thing, I hain't been neighborly, that's a fact. But they're such dreadful proud people, I hated to go near 'em."

"Now, Melissy, like as not, they're no more stuck up than other folks, jist because they keep a man to help 'em."

"Law, it's so queer, he does house-work, and all kinds. He told me he was going to try to do the ironin' himself, for he said his lady didn't know no more about it than a baby, I kinder thought he wanted me to offer to hire out to 'em to do it; but I never hired out, even when I was a girl, and I'm certain I shan't do it now."

"I saw Mr. Lancaster, that's the gentleman, yesterday, and had quite a talk with him. I felt right sorry for him, he was so downcast, though he didn't say so. He was askin' me something about sowing wheat this fall. He knows as much about farmin' as his wife does about ironin'. What, in the name of sense, brought such people out here, is more'n I can guess."

The nearer approach of the individual they were watching put a stop to their remarks. Peter Potter, could not but smile, as he observed the mincing steps and nice precision of the man, who came up to them, looking so fine in his long-tailed coat of blue broadcloth, with black breeches and buckled shoes, that Mrs. Potter felt at once that he must look with contempt upon the check trowsers and red flannel shirt of her Peter. But the mincing steps of their visitor had become such second nature to him, that he practiced them at all times, and it was evident that he was now too greatly flurried to think of himself. He was a little fellow, not over five feet two, and of an undefinable age, he might be forty, fifty, or sixty, but his iron-gray hair, his thin, small face, and wiry figure, told no satisfactory story on this subject.

"My master and mistress be both in trouble," he exclaimed, in answer to the squatter's "how-d'ye-do." "If you'd both of you come over, especially the woman, you'd do us a great favor," and he ended his appeal with a groan.

" What's the matter? sickness?" asked the Potters, rising,
and showing in their countenances at once that sympathy
which alone makes settlers' lives endurable.

" Sickness!   O Lord, yes.   Both of them.   There's something very strange the matter with master.   He's all of a
tremble—his teeth chatter—his lips are blue—his legs shake—
and he says he's freezing, and here it is, as you know, sir, a
day fit to melt folks.   O Lord, that ever we should have
come to a country like this."

" It's nothing to be scart about, though it's mighty dis-
agreeable, and I'm right sorry the gentleman's took it.   It's
nothing but fever 'n agcr, most everybody has it in these
parts, till they wear it out."

" But that isn't the worst," continued the servant.   " Mistress has been trying to do things she was never brought up
to do, and she's taking with great distress now, though it's not
her time.   But I think the woman will know better than I
what to do for her—and if she's any hand to help in such cases,
I pray her to go quick to my poor lady."

" For the Lord's sake! you don't say so!   Peter, you call
them young ones in, and give 'em their supper and put 'em to
bed.   Then you can come over, and bring along the yarb-bag.
I'm going right straight off this minute."

And right straight off she went, so fast, that the little anxious old man, by her side, had to run to keep up with her.
Once he caught his feet in the tangled grass and fell; but his
only remark as he rubbed his knees, and hurried along was—

" O Lord, that ever we should have come to a country
like this."

" Where did you come from?" Mrs. Potter found time to
inquire.

" H'england, *of course.*"

The cabin which Mrs. Potter found herself approaching,
was one which had been erected by a family the same season
of their own settlement, who had afterward grown so homesick that they had abandoned it and returned to the East.   It
was hidden from view of their own dwelling by one of those
rolling hills which diversified the surface of the prairie, and
was about a mile distant.   She had often been in it when the
other family remained there.   It was of better construction

than their own shanty, which had but one large room, this having two tolerable rooms and a loft above. The first settler in it had been a person of taste, who had taken great pains to transplant all kinds of beautiful, climbing wild-vines under its windows; and these had now grown until the rough outside of the house was covered with bloom That handsomest of roses, the queen of the prairie, was now in full blossom over the front, and the woman could hardly refrain from pausing a moment to admire it. But the thought of the critical condition of the strange lady within hastened her steps.

She threw up her hands as she stepped in at the front door. She gave but a glance at the curious mingling of refinement and poverty which met her gaze—the casket of jewels, the fine lace handkerchief, the elegant books scattered upon a table hewn with the ax roughly out of the cottonwood of the prairie. Hastening to the side of the rude bed, she took the cold hands, so small and white, of the sufferer lying there, chafing them with real, motherly tenderness. A face of girlish beauty and innocence won her love the moment she looked on it. So forlorn, so pitiable it was, to find one so delicate, so young, suffering so much, and under such circumstances.

Sitting upon the other side of the bed was the husband, now in a high fever after his severe chill, but utterly regardless of his own feelings in his great anxiety about the condition of his wife.

That night was one of misery never to be forgotten. Day light found Mrs. Potter walking the floor distractedly with a feeble infant in her arms; the young father of which knelt silently, gazing at the dead mother. The cheeks, which but yesterday were brilliant with the health of an English girl, would never blush again—all was changed, save the bright, brown hair, floating over the pillow so lustrous, as beautiful as ever.

Mrs. Potter, stranger though she was, was heart-broken at the terrible tragedy. The poor little puny face of the babe she carried was wet with the tears which rolled from her eyes. James, the servant, had folded his dead lady's hands, smoothed back her hair, straightened the covering of the bed, as calmly, apparently, as he would have laid the cloth for dinner. But Mrs. Potter saw that a tremor shook him all the time, and that he did not weep because he could not. Then he spoke to his master, trying to rouse him from the appalling trance into which he had fallen; but at present he would not be disturbed, and the noon-time came and the night before any sound or tear escaped him.

The kindness of the Potters won the confidence of the quaint old serving-man, so that, during the sad days of the death and burial, they found out some of the circumstances which had brought a family of this kind to so uncongenial a place. .

Edith Thorntou was the daughter of a clergyman of high repute, residing in Edinburgh. In loveliness of mind and person, and in accomplishments, she was the equal of any of the daughters of rank with whom she frequently associated by means of the honored position of her father. But she was neither wealthy nor titled—therefore she was not considered eligible in the match-making "Old Country."

Edwin Lancaster was the son of a very wealthy English family, who were ambitious that his fine person and great fortune should secure him a titled wife, and who were, of course, disappointed at their darling's falling in love with a clergyman's daughter, and set their countenance most rigidly against the match. On the other hand, Mr. Thornton had his objections—for Edwin Lancaster had been rather wild—and he had also too much pride to wish an alliance with a family who did not themselves desire it. So the young people met with nothing but opposition; the consequence of which was that they ran away, were married, and, very full of love and hope, set sail for America, believing that here plenty could be had for the asking, and with their heads full of the romance of "love in a cottage."

It was here that James, an old family servant of the Lancasters, who had been deeply attached to Edwin from a child, finding that his master was not going to recall the runaways, came after them, and devoted himself to their service, without prospect of much other present reward than the privilege of attending upon his pet boy.

For nearly a year they tarried in New York. Mr. Lancaster obtained a situation, at a moderate salary, in a public library, and his wife gave a few lessons in music. So the young

couple might have prospered tolerably, and lived, as new be-
ginners in America expect to live, nicely and comfortably, had
not Edwin began to grow impatient. He had expected a recall, or, at least, a remittance from his father; and when none
came he grew embittered. Not even his deep love for the
most heroic, most devoted, and most lovely of all sweet wives
could keep this bitterness out of his heart. The monotony
and privation of his life grew more and more distasteful to
him; while, with the pride and passion of his impulsive nature, he resolved upon getting rich—so rich that the immensity
of his fortune should enable him to hurl back the scorn of his
selfish relatives. A want both of capital and experience was
not just the requisites for securing this expected wealth in a
city crowded with keen and eager competitors; and hearing
some marvelous, exaggerated accounts of the prosperous West,
he persuaded Edith to be of his mind, threw up his situation,
exchanging certainty for uncertainty at a very critical period
in their lives. The money necessary for the enterprize was
obtained by the sale of nearly all of Edith's jewelry, added to
a hundred pounds her father had inclosed to her in his last
letter as a present to the little-expected stranger, who would,
doubtless, even in its first worldly experience, find a hundred
pounds quite serviceable.

Discouraged by several attempts to get into business in
some of the thriving villages along his route, in love with the
beauty of the prairie, and trying to believe, with his sweet,
enthusiastic Edith, that the wild, free life of the West, and
the romance of that untenanted, rose-covered cabin would satisfy them for the present, and that, at least, it was only pru-
dent to find some stopping-place before their child was born,
they had finally found shelter in this out-of-the-way spot,
where, happy in each other, they were waiting for the future.

Here it was that all the surprising resources of James had
come into play. Proud and particular as any old English
family servant could be, his affection for the young couple got
the better of most of his scruples; he cooked, washed, and had
attempted to iron. He had made them mattresses of prairie-
hay, chopped and whittled out various articles of furniture;
he had traveled on foot twelve miles to the nearest village
and hired a wagon to come out with groceries and such stores
as were to be found in that small, new settlement.

But alas! for all his loving toil. Sickness, that worst scourge of the western emigrant, laid its hand very soon upon their happiness. Edith, so young, so inexperienced, was unfitted for the trials which came upon her. She came to that wide, wild prairie to find a grave there, instead of the cunning home her hope had pictured.

Mr. Lancaster gave up at once all thought of life in America. The great solitude of the prairie threatened, in his mood, to destroy his mind. He could not bear it. He resolved to return to the home of his youth. He wished to take his child; but that was simply impossible, for the present. Mrs. Potter promised to do her best by it, and he had faith in her word; it was a little girl, and she had no daughter—she should love it as if it were hers. James, faithful to the last degree, declared his intention of remaining with the child, and serving it, until his master's return for it, which was to be as soon as it was considered old enough to bear the journey. A year was the time set.

CHAPTER II.

AND thus it had been that the little Edith came to the squatter's cabin. She was a lovely little creature, and grew plump and promising under the tender, pitying care she received—full pretty enough for the grand-daughter of an English commoner, and full sturdy enough for the home of an Illinois squatter. Take her all in all—anteeedents, birth, and prospects—she made the very good beginning of a heroine; and to hint at the destiny before her, let us say that she had two devoted lovers before she was a month old—Daniel and Amos Potter, aged seven and six years respectively, who quarreled for her smiles, and tore each other's hair in her defence.

The year which followed was a long and lonely year for poor James. He boarded himself in his own house, but the greater part of every day was spent in carrying the baby around in his arms, and which was a great relief to Mrs. Potter, who had plenty of work on hand. The baby, in its beautiful, soft garments, embroidered by the fingers now moldering into dust, made a pretty picture, attended upon by the quaint old servitor. The patience of a mother could not exceed his patience in all matters pertaining to the child; but in other affairs he was petulant and unreasonable, and annoyed good, patriotic Mrs. Potter exceedingly, by exclaiming twenty times a day, on every and all occasions:

"O Lord, that ever I should 'ave come to a country like this!"

There was an Indian station some forty miles from there, and the Indians crossed that prairie every fall, on their way to the station, where they were paid their government allowance.

"I've never seen one of your American savages," remarked James, one day, as he sat on Mrs. Potter's "settle," holding little Edith on his knee, and watching the housewife stewing "punkin" for pies. 'I've heard so much of them, that I've a great curiosity to see them"

"Wouldn't you be afraid?" asked Mrs. Potter, who had not much respect for the bravery contained in the bosom of the blue coat.

"Afraid! who ever knew a Hinglishman to be afraid of any thing under the sun, ma'am, I'd like to know? You do not happreciate us."

"Possibly. But Peter thought you was a little scared the time you and him met the b'ar."

"Oh well, law, ma'am, a bear is a very different thing from a Hindian. I own I was a little flustered, but it was simply because the event was so unexpected. I've never been accustomed to bears. They do not have any such houtrageous monsters in Hingland. However, if I'd ever known he was a coming, and had a been prepared, I presume I shouldn't 'ave flinched."

"Wall, I'm free to own I don't like the Injins; they're a snaky set. Peter says your coat-tails stood out straight that time the b'ar growled, and stuck his head out that holler tree."

"I took to flight, of course, but I was actuated by no—gracious!"

Mrs. Potter looked up from stewing her pumpkin, and her eyes fell upon at least one hundred dusky savages who had stolen silently in front of the house. James gave one jump, with Edith in his arms, and got behind the portly form of Mrs. Potter. The unwelcome visitors thought this a good joke, and set up yells and shrieks of delight, brandishing their guns and bows, dancing, and making uncouth gestures.

"Don't let 'em see you're afraid," spoke Mrs. Potter, in a low voice—she herself had hardly changed countenance—"or p'r'aps they'll be a little sassy. There's no reason to be scared. They've been up to the station, and are on their way home. They're friendly tribes; I know 'em."

Saying this, she seated herself in the door, and looked composedly at them. Seeing they could not frighten her, they ceased to brandish their weapons, and gathered close about.

"O Lord, that ever we should 'ave come to a country like

this!" she heard James whispering to himself from the farthest corner of the room.

Some of the Indians who could talk a little English asked for fire-water. She told them she had none, but knew they had plenty, for they had just come from the station. Then they showed her the trinkets and new clothes they had received. Twenty or thirty squaws stood in the background with papooses and sacks of corn on their backs. The whole party seemed in the best of humors, jingling the money in the wampum bags they had fastened to their belts. Several of them pushed past Mrs. Potter into the cabin. She allowed them to do as they pleased; but upon looking round for James, he was nowhere to be seen. A smothered cry from little Edith betrayed his hiding-place, and with a whoop of devilish mischief, the savages overturned the stick bedstead, betraying the poor little Englishman crouched ignominiously under it, his handkerchief stuffed in the baby's mouth.

Nothing could now restrain the fun of the Indians, whose contempt for cowardice is always so strong. A gray-headed old chief took little Edith in his arms very carefully, and looked on, while a dozen others seized their victim, pulling him about unmercifully, twisting their hands in the hair which he, unfortunately, wore long, and making motions as if about to scalp him. He shut his eyes and gave himself up for dead. Mrs. Potter knew they would not dare to seriously injure him, it being their policy to keep on good terms with government; and she could hardly keep from feeling an uncharitable triumph over the boastful person who so often made her feel his contempt for American institutions generally, and herself in particular. Yet she heartily wished her Peter was at home, as he could have driven off their rude visitors with one or two firm words.

When they had fingered every article in the room, and tormented James until he was nearly insensible, and firmly believed himself dead, they began to withdraw, the old chief taking the infant with him. Mrs. Potter went and took it from him. He yielded it up very reluctantly; but came back and offered fifty cents for it, then a dollar, then more, adding a few shillings at a time, until the sum reached five dollars. When she still smilingly refused all, he gave a grunt of despair

and stalked off.   Looking after them, to see if they stolen any ſ
thing, she immediately missed the ax and a hammer which
had been lying by the wood-pile, and running after them, she
threatened them with informing the great father at Washington
of the loss of the chattels, if they did not give them up.

"I'll confess, ma'am, you're a woman of spirit," murmured
James, when he saw her return with the missing implements.
"Were you not afraid they would use the ax to make way
with you?   Did you see how near I came to losing my life?
If I hadn't 'ave fought 'em so long as I had breath, I shouldn't
be alive now, to talk about it.   They sneaked off when they
saw how determined I was.   But my coat's tore, and I'm all
bruised up.   O Lord, that ever I should 'ave come to a country like this!   Next time I write to master I _ca_ inform him
of the danger we've been in, and the efforts I _made_ to conceal
his child from the savages by hiding her under the bed.   I
shall advise him to come quickly and rescue us from the
dangers which beset us in this 'ere wild region."

"Wall, you've seen Injins, now, and felt 'em, too; and I
guess you're not so curious about 'em as you was a spell ago.
I see very plain you're a dangerous man in a fight, Mr.
Pipkin," and Mrs. Potter laughed good-naturedly.   "Take
off your coat, and I'll set down and mend it for you.   I never
purtended to like Injins.   They're a pesky, thieving set; and
ugly where they durst to be.   But you don't catch me backing
out, and letting 'em carry off the only ax Peter's got.   As for
your writing to Mr. Lancaster, I suppose he'll come in the due
course of time; and I, for one, shall be sorry to see him.
That baby seems as much my own, exactly as if I'd brought
it into the world, and it'll be a mournful day for me when it
goes out from under my roof."

"You've been uncommon good to my babe, ma'am—just as
good as a foster-mother could be; you've made it flourish on
cow's milk as fine as if it had its own proper element," answered James, softened alike by the mending process going on
with his coat, and the thought of the devotion of the whole
family to his darling; "but as for your talking about its being
yours—lawk, anybody can see it's a Lancaster all over.   She's
the picture of her father a'ready.   She's going to be a great
lady, this little infant is, ma'am.   She'll wear jewels only

second to Queen Victory, and ride a horseback and in a car-riage-and-four, and have everybody a-coming at her bidding."

"Maybe she will, Mr. Pipkin; but I'll tell you how it seems to me. It seems as if that child was never going to leave this cabin—not as long as it stands, or we live in it. There, now, you know just what's in my mind. It's pre-sentiment."

Just then Mr. Potter entered with his little boys, who had been permitted to accompany him to the village, where he had been to dispose of some of his corn and obtain groceries in exchange, he being now the fortunate possessor of a horse and wagon, which he had purchased with money forced upon him by Mr. Lancaster, before his departure. He held in his hand a letter for James, which proved to be from his master, the first he had received, and this was sent back from ship-board by a passing vessel, for passages in those days were not made in eight or ten days. The letter was brief, but eloquent with solicitude and love for the little waif thrown so strangely upon a western prairie.

This letter proved to be the last as well as the first. Whether the voyage was never completed, and the master perished by fire or shipwreck, or what event or calamity had caused that long, long dreary silence, could only be guessed. The year set for his absence passed, and another followed on, and poor old James' eyes were blurred and strained with constant watching for an arrival which never took place. We have called the silence long and dreary; it was so only to the anxious, home-sick servitor. No more children came to the Potters; and their affections became so fondly fixed upon the beautiful little creature who brightened their cabin, that they dreaded nothing so much as that looked-for parent who should snatch their treasure from them.

"The boys wouldn't know nothing what to do without that child, especially Amos, who just dotes on her; and as for Peter, she believed he'd just be broke down. He was so fond of girl babies; his whole heart was sot on that child," mused the good woman a thousand times, as her eyes followed the little one.

She made just such check-aprons and woolen gowns for the dainty Miss Edith as she would have done for a daughter

of her own ; and the prim attendant groaned in spirit to see
the lovely little heiress of the Lancasters playing with the pigs,
and, what was just as bad in his estimation, her *brothers* Dan
and Amos eating with a pewter spoon out of an earthern mug,
and relishing a corn-dodger in blissful ignorance of the superior merits of English plum-pudding.

"I don't see why you need to run this country down, in
particular," remarked Mr. Potter to the querulous James upon
one occasion ; "you're gettin' to be a rich man and a landed
próprietor, which, I reckon, wouldn't have happened to you
if you'd staid where you belonged. Don't grumble over your
good luck, old fellow."

James straightened himself as tall as his five feet two inches
would permit, and looked around grandly upon his estate.
The Potters and himself had been steadily and swiftly whirled
up the wheel of fortune during the few years of their acquaintance.

Finding that grieving after his master would not bring him
back, James had taken possession of all the land the government allowed him, both for himself and Edith. Of this, at
first, he cultivated but little, but he went into the business of
market-gardener ; and very glad were the new settlers in
Beaver-Creek village, who had money to buy with, to take his
vegetables and fruits at high prices.

Gradually he had hired men to plant wheat and corn for
him ; he had apple and peach trees growing and bearing
fruit; and the vine-covered cabin which he occupied took on
an air of English rural life and comfort. His pig-pens were
out of sight of the house, in front of which he had a beautiful
flower-garden, and in the rear the large vegetable-gardens from
which he made so much money. In striking contrast to the
Potter's flowerless and shrubless home was James's snug resi-
dence. Mrs. Potter was neat indoors and a thriving housewife, but she had little taste for the refinements of life.

The devotion of the old servant to the child of Edith was
something pleasant to see. It was for her he raised flowers;
for her he fixed up the front room so finely with white curtains and a carpet; for her he bought an Indian pony; for
her even that he laid up money. He had taken her home to
live with him, and to "try and make a lady of her."

It was the trial of his life that she *would* play with " them Potters," just as if she wasn't the heiress of the Lancasters.

Obedient as she was, and fond of " her James," it was impossible to prevent her running away, every day of her life, to bask in the sunshiny presence of Mrs. Potter, with the boys, the pigs, the dog, and great, strong Mr. Potter, who could swing her up to the very ceiling, and carry her all around on his shoulder.

"If she hadn't a been born in such a country as this, where there wasn't no kings and queens, and never a lord or a lady to gladden the eyes, she wouldn't never take to sliding down straw-stacks, chasing the chickens, and sitting on top a rail fence," he groaned, inwardly.

Certain it is, that if she had not been just as buoyant and thoughtless as she was, his training would have made a very vain and silly girl of her. He would bring her home from her romps with the boys, set her up primly in the pretty chair he had bought her, and talk to her by the hour about the necessity of her preparing herself to be a very wonderful young lady some time.

Edith used to like to listen to the story of her future prospects; England was fairy-land to her; her unknown father was a fairy prince, with unlimited jewels and splendid clothes at his command. The part of the history which touched her the most deeply was the death of her beautiful mother; she knew her grave, and assisted James in keeping the flowers in perfect order which covered it. Another part of the story which she liked, was when James, the more graphically to enforce his theory of properties, drew forth from a chest which he kept carefully locked, pearls which he clasped about her throat and arms, and a jeweled brooch which he pinned in her little, homespun gown, and showed her the miniatures of a beautiful couple—her own father and mother, telling her she must be like them.

She would climb upon the table before the looking-glass and admire the splendor in which she was arrayed, unconscious that her rosy, dimpled cheeks, bright ringlets, and happy eyes were far lovelier than the ornaments she wore. Try hard as he might, he could not spoil a nature as joyous as hers; and the dreams which sometimes fixed those blue eyes in rev-eric, were only just deep enough to soften and shadow her sunny temperament.

In the mean time the boys were growing up into young men. Two or three winters they had been away to the village academy, returning home and working with their father through the farming-season. Daniel, the eldest, was like his mother, a person of good, sound sense and very little romance, tall, and good-looking. Amos was more like his father, sharp and shrewd enough, but with an undeveloped amount of fine, generous feeling and poetic perception added to it. He was eminently handsome, too, despite of his brown hands and sunburnt cheeks. He wore his wammus and straw-hat with a grace of his own, which nothing could disfigure.

He was little Edith's teacher. James was obliged to confess that Amos could teach the little one her Ha-B, Habs, better than he could. She liked to get out under the shade of a tree, or upon the broad, top rail of the fence and study beside of Amos. He took her beyond her a-b abs, into reading and geography, arithmetic and history. He repeated to her some of the facts of astronomy, learning her to trace the constellations.

James fretted more and more as time passed on, and no harp or piano, no drawing-master, no dancing-master, no silver forks nor Sevres toilet-sets were to be had for his little lady.

Between James and Amos there was growing up more and more of a dislike. The boy was too proud to brook the evident thought of the old man, that he was not good enough to associate with his charge. He knew Edith liked him, and that they had famous times together.

"Oh, you needn't be taking her off in that style," he said once, tauntingly; "she's going to be my wife some time; so you might as well be letting her get used to me."

"*Your* wife! you haudacious young clodhopper, you! How durst you—you—you—talk so to a Lancaster?"

"You needn't get out of patience and stutter so. Edith's promised; haven't you, little one? I think she will make me a very passable wife, if she keeps on growing pretty so fast."

"Come right straight home, Edith Lancaster, and don't never speak to that bold, bad, vulgar fellow again. Your father will be very much displeased when he hears of it"

" Her father seems to take a great interest in her, don't he, now? I'm afraid she'll get to be an old, old maid if she waits to marry one of the English dukes or princes you have in store for her. And look here, if you're not more polite, I shall take the little lady away from you—eh, Edith ?"

Enraged beyond endurance by this audacity, the little old man started off so blindly that he ran over a monstrous sow, who was crunching wormy apples under the trees, who took him on her back and trotted off with him, giving him a fine John-Gilpin ride around and around the orchard, Edith clap-ping her hands and applauding the performance merrily.

" O Lord, that ever I should 'ave come to a country like this !" sighed James, as he picked himself up.

" You may go back to Hold Hingland as quick as you please, after I marry this little girl," was the consoling remark of Amos.

This trifling adventure was the means of bringing James Pipkin to a resolution he had long hesitated to make—and that was to send Edith to the Beaver Creek young ladies' school. He not only dreaded to part with her; but he had an indistinct idea that her father, if she still had a father, would not like it. But to leave her where she was, under the unlimited influence of the Potter's, was not to be thought of by him. Besides, it was high time, if she was ever going to have any accomplishments, that she should begin the acquire-ment of them.

" Don't spare no pains nor expense. She must have the best," was his parting injunction to the lady with whom, one spring morning, he left his inconsolable charge, frightened and forlorn, at the new sphere in which she found herself.

" Let her go," muttered Amos; " all the better. I can study as well as she. I shall tell father, now, that I want more time for schooling."

It was but a brief time after this that he had a private talk with his father, the result of which was that he prepared him-self to leave home and enter school at the East. His parents were now abundantly able to afford him this privilege. He had worked side by side with his father for years, and felt that a portion of his earnings ought to be his, for the purpose of enabling him to fit himself to take a higher rank among

men.   Mr. Potter was too sagacious a man, and had craved
"book·larning" too earnestly himself, not to be proud of this
disposition in his son, and ready to furnish him with means.

Daniel concluded that his education was already sufficient
for his purposes; he was of a speculative turn, and had obtained an interest in some valuable lead-mines then being
opened in the country north of theirs.

So the Potters were now quite alone in the new house they
had built, and Mr. Pipkin was undisturbed in the pursuance
of that thrifty acquisitiveness which was gradually filling his
chest with coin, and which enabled him to pay all the bills of
the boarding·school with a flourish quite to his liking.

The original old blue coat still hung upon him, though he had
a new one made after the same pattern, to wear when he vis-
ited the child in whom he took such a quaint and unselfish
pride.

"I belongs to her, ma'am," he informed the lady-principal,
"as I belonged to her grandfather and her father.   It shan't
never be said that one of the Lancasters was without a follower."

The history of the child became known in the school, and
made her quite a heroine; but she bore her honors meekly.

CHAPTER III

THE YOUNG ARTISTS—JAMES' NARRATIVE.

EDITH had been four years at school. In those four years she had grown into maidenhood; she was little Edith no longer. The most lovely and beloved of the pupils at the seminary, the pride of the principal upon all occasions of public display, and the heroine of a hundred romantic stories, she still pined for some one *to belong to*, some one who would call her daughter, and receive the lavish affection of her heart.

It was a very dangerous state for a young lady's heart to be in—this craving after love and confidence. Such stores of affection lying ready to be given away, would be very apt to have somebody to beg them; and if their proper owner did not appear to claim them, some interloper might receive what had been accumulating for the benefit of that mysterious, unknown father, the ideal of manhood to her imagination. Amos Potter, studying hard in a distant State, and laying up a sweet thought of her with every honor he won, did not think much of this danger. Occasionally he wrote her a letter beginning with "*Dear* Edith;" to which she responded in a pretty, gossiping way, beginning hers, "Dear brother."

One Saturday in May, Edith had permission to spend the holiday at home. James had brought in her pony for her to ride out, and Mrs. Potter had sent her word that she must come there to dinner, for they'd killed the fatted calf, and were going to have veal pot-pie.

As she cantered out of the village, which now had a long row of handsome cottages stretching out into the country, with her satchel containing a supply of drawing-materials for company, her heart exulted in fullness of youth and life. James followed at a respectful distance behind, on a horse of his own, marking, with admiring eyes, the lovely form and easy grace of his youthful mistress. He looked not a day older than he had done sixteen years before; he was just as weazen, just as prim, and his breeches and coat looked as if they might be the old, identical ones. They stopped at Mrs. Potter's, and then James went on with the horses, while Edith put off her chat with the housewife until dinner, as she had taken a fancy to sketch the scenery about her home. After looking about a little, she chose a seat near the spring, in a little bower which had always been a favorite spot with her; from here she had a view of a range of distant bluffs, the sweeping expanse of prairie, and the house and orchard near at hand. Her seat was a mossy stone, looking like a great emerald set in a sapphire ring, so thickly was it clustered about by violets. Flinging her bonnet aside, she gathered two or three early wild-roses, out of pure love of them, sticking them in her hair and bosom.

"Now, child, to work!" she said, addressing herself, as she drew forth pencils and drawing-book.

Steadily she worked away, the color deepening in her cheek with the glow of satisfactory progression, utterly lost to every thing but her absorbing employment. She had labored over an hour, when she paused to rest, throwing off her weariness in a long sigh; then, tossing back the bright profusion of her hair, she glanced around to take in the whole beautiful prospect.

Uttering an exclamation under her breath, she grew almost pale with the sudden start.

She was not the only artist who was out that morning Not forty feet from where she had been sitting so coolly and contentedly, for so long a time, sat a young gentleman, engaged like herself, in sketching. He was comfortably seated upon a camp-stool, to which was attached a sliding box, containing the necessary appurtenances for drawing in watercolors or with crayons. At the moment when she discovered him, he was in such a position as showed plainly that she was his subject.

"The impertinent fellow!" she murmured.

He was looking down upon his work when she discovered him; and when he looked up, instead of looking at her, as she expected, his clear blue eyes darted their firm rays directly upon the distant bluff.

"Perhaps he had not put her in his picture after all; how she would like to know," and Edith tied on her bonnet, affecting not to see the stranger, gathered up her portfolio, and retreated to the house.

"Wall," said Mrs. Potter, as she made her appearance, "your pictur' and the pot-pie are done at the same time. Dinner's just ready; I'll blow the horn for the men, and we'll set right down."

The men! Edith knew of but one man at present belonging to the premises. She asked no questions, but waited for the summons to dinner to gratify her curiosity in due time.

Mr. Potter came in presently, shaking hands with her, according to custom, and hoping to find her flourishing.

"Whar's the stranger?" asked the wife, as they drew their chairs to the table.

"Comin'," replied the host, as he plunged a knife into the pot-pie.

"I forgot to tell you, sis," went on Mrs. Potter, "there was a stranger staid with us last night—a right good-lookin', well-spoken young man—a picture-maker, like you. He got belated from reaching the village, a drawin' this place and things round here, and asked leave to stop till he was through. We don't know nothing about him, but we've never turned anybody from the door yet, 'less they were drunk. I guess he'll be around all day."

"Comin'" the stranger was, for at that moment he entered the door, doffing his straw hat with well-bred ease, and setting his camp-stool down in a corner.

"Miss Lancaster, I'll make ye acquainted with Mr. Beverly."

Edith made her coldest, most queenly bow. Nevertheless, she detected the slightest hint of a mischievous smile in the eyes of her new acquaintance, which belied the polite gravity of the rest of his countenance. He sat down to dinner.

"Did you and Miss Lancaster see each other when you was out? I reckoned you'd meet."

"I saw the lady; I can not say whether she saw me or not."

Edith made no reply, being occupied with her plate.

"You've both such a likin' for rambling about and making pictures, I expect you'll take to each other," continued friendly.

innocent Mrs. Potter. "Two artists, as you call yourselves, at my table, I s'pose I ought to feel honored."

The stranger smiled. There was just the slightest haughty motion of the young girl's head, which told of innate aristocracy, and she kept her eyes carefully from his direction.

"Pshaw!" growled Mr. Potter. "Seems to me pencils and paper and such like puttering trash is small work for men— not but making picters is pretty enough work for girls. Hope you'll excuse me, stranger, but them's my sentiments."

Edith caught the young gentleman's eye, and laughed out in her sweet, merry way.

"Do not make any apologies for being severe upon us; we are used to it," replied the stranger. "We know it's the fashion of the world to think there's common-sense in nothing but money-making."

"Wall, how are we to get along without money, I'd like to know? If the men don't make money, what will the women do, hey, sis?"

"Oh, don't ask me! I'm sure I never thought," cried Edith. "James gives me all I want, and that's all I care about it."

"About as much as women in gineral know," growled the host, with a laugh.

A general good humor prevailed at the close of the meal; after which Mr. Beverly asked Edith to see her sketch.

"With pleasure, if I may see yours in return."

Mrs. Potter bent over it, to look at it with her.

"Law, if he hasn't got you in, as natural as your own face," she exclaimed, delightedly. "Did you set still and let him take you."

"She sat very still," said the artist, with a spice of enjoyment in his tone. "She scarcely stirred for over an hour. Just the position I liked, too. See how exquisite the profile is, and the graceful bend of her head; while the pencil in her hand and the sketch in her lap, gave her an artistic air, highly becoming to my picture."

"Thank you for flattering me through a medium," answered Edith, half-vexed and half-amused. "I do not think I should have kept so still if I had known the consequences. I shall only forgive your presumption upon condition that you give me the painting."

"I do not ask your forgiveness," said he, with that careless proud, and yet gay manner, which scarcely displeases because of its frank independence. "I am privileged to sketch nature wherever I find her beautiful, and if there are accessories to the landscape which render it yet more charming, am I to blame for that?"

Edith had no refuge except in the case of drawings. Any remark of hers only called forth fresh compliment from the audacious artist. She saw by his sketches and his water-color drawings, that he was an artist of unusual merit; and found, in the course of a brief conversation, that he was English, was a landscape-painter by profession, and was making a tour through America for the sole purpose of sketching some of its most striking scenery.

While they were yet lingering over the portfolio, James came in to ask Edith to walk over to her own cottage and see the new flower-beds he had been marking out. A nervous trepidation seized him as soon as he recognized one of his own countrymen; a hope to hear some tidings of his master occasioned it; and he insisted, with an earnestness unlike his usual small pomposity, upon the gentleman accompanying him to see "his place."

Very glad was the stranger of this chance of prolonging his interview with the lovely girl whose face would make so sweet a picture. As she hastened before them, eager to see the improvements in her flower-garden, James took the opportunity of telling her history to the young gentleman whose profession brought him in contact with so many wealthy families; but Mr. Beverly had never had the honor of being patronized by the Lancasters, and knew nothing of them.

His interest in her beauty was increased by the little story the old man told him; and he promised, upon his return to London, to make inquiries, and if he learned any thing, to write to Mr. Pipkin.

"It's awful to see a Lancaster growin' up in a country like this," groaned James, his long-repressed sorrows flowing forth into the ear of a fellow-countryman. "I've lain awake nights and thought of it, and fancied I heard my master's steps comin' up to the door, my heart was so full of it. I've done the best I could by her, bein' placed as I were,—and I must say she's no disgrace to her family, if she were brought up in an 'owling western wilderness. I must say, if it *is* all my own work, as it were, that she's a very 'andsome and 'igh-bred young lady, that they won't be ashamed of when she gets her own."

"I must say, Mr. Pipkin, that you have indeed done wonders," responded his listener, with a smile. "I do not think any duchess or countess whose portrait has graced the walls of our academy was ever better brought up, to say nothing of her beauty."

"Lord, though, but I were distressed about her musical hedecation, and her drawing and dancing and other haccomplishments; but she's getting along finely now, sir; she can play like a hangel and sing like a nightingale—four years she's been at it now. I've sold vegetables of all kinds, and put myself hout a great deal to pay her schooling; there's no telling the bushels of carrots and turnips, the bunches of hasparagus and rhubarb, and the wagon-loads of cabbages, and all kinds, that's gone into her hedecation."

"She'll belong to the school of vegetarians then, I suppose?"

"Well, I don't know as to that, sir,—it's a very nice school for this country, which isn't saying much. If you'd 'ave seen the country when we first come to it, you'd a wondered how we could 'ave survived, being Lancasters as we were and used to the best. Lord, sir, I killed a bear myself!—a hatrocious beast, he was, who stuck his 'ead out of an 'oller tree and growled at me and Potter, as we were a passing by. When Potter see him coming down and roaring like a lion, he dropped his gun and run; but I picked up the gun and looked the hanimal straight in the eye, and when he saw that he kind of stopped, and I give him the ball, and he fell dead."

"Mr. Potter didn't look to me like a man who would run from a bear. I should have thought *you* would have been the person not to stand your ground. You're so small, you know, and not accustomed to bears."

"Happearances are very deceptive, sir. I know I'm small, but I'm tough—and you never knew a Lancaster, or a follower of a Lancaster, that wasn't brave. We're a fighting race, sir. Lord! I could make your hair stand on end, if I'd tell you 'alf. When that young lady, sir, was a hinfaut in harms, and I carried her about from morning till night, and did every thing for her but just furnish her her nourishment, we were sett-ng peaceably over at Mrs. Potter's, and he away, when we were surprised by several hundred bloody Indians, who sur-rounded the 'ouse with their tomahawks and knives, yelling like jinfernal fiends and brandishing their weapons and firebrands— and there was never a bolt to the door, and only a single-barreled rifle in the 'ouse. I tell you, sir, I thought our time had come. I just pushed Mrs. Potter and the baby under the bed; and then a thought seized me. Potter had a small can-nister he'd just brought home, with a couple of pounds of powder in it, and I cotched that and rushed out into the thickest of 'em, all the while they striking at me and whoop-ing; and I poured out the powder and touched it off with a coal from the fireplace, which I threw out the window, and it went off and blew forty or fifty of 'em up, and frightened the rest so they run like deer. I tell you it shook the windows right out of the 'ouse and knocked the chimney down. One Indian was blowed right through the door. O Lord, but me and Potter had a time burying them dead savages! I was sick enough of the country, I tell you; and if I hadn't been looking for my master, I'd have taken my baby on my back and started for 'ome."

"A very thrilling adventure, indeed, Mr, Pipkin."

"Me and Potter put up a pen to catch wild turkeys, and I went out alone hearly one morning to see if there were any game, and a wolf who'd been after the turkeys got after me. He was so close once that he bit off the tail of my coat—not this one, the one I wore over—but I can show you the place —but I climbed up a tree, and there I staid, he a 'owling around the trunk of it, till Potter came out to see what was the fuss. I've seen perilous times, I tell you, sir."

"You have, indeed, for a man of your size."

"I didn't care so much for my own danger, and none of the comforts of civilized life, as I did to see my young lady a-growing up a heating mush with a pewter spoon, or a wearing pinafores made of the same as Mrs. Potter's check haprons. I used to take her aside and tell her 'ow to 'old her fork; and that a Lancaster young lady had never been seen to make dirt-pies, or to ride the pig; and I used to be 'orribly shocked at the fondness she had for playing with them boys, and behaving herself like a Hamerican. It's the only thing she was ever self-willed about. I told her I didn't think her father would be pleased at her taking to them Potters so; but she told me she couldn't 'elp it if he wasn't; she couldn't 'elp loving them, and she shouldn't try. And she didn't."

Just at this epoch in the loquacious little man's story, they reached the garden-gate, where Edith stood, looking too fresh and brilliant and beautiful to have any trace of the dirt-pies of her childhood left about her; unless it was in the roses of her cheeks, which were certainly the brighter for such unlovely employment in times gone by.

James pointed out the improvements he had made, turning the cabin into an English cottage, and making the wilderness of prairie to blossom like a rose; in corroboration of his story, he showed the grave of Edith's mother, the room in which she died, the jewels and portraits left in his possession.

By this time it was growing toward sunset, and as the artist had to return to Beaver-Creek village that evening, he tore himself away from the romantic spot in which he had been so interested, and with a lingering, regretful gaze of intense admiration at the blushing Edith, bade her farewell.

This little chance incident, so trifling in itself, was destined to have more than a passing influence upon our heroine's history.

CHAPTER IV.

UNCLE EZEKIEL.

"O LORD, that ever I should 'ave come to such a country as this!"

Amos and Edith had been out, gathering the delicious wild plums which grew in their latitude. They were both home from school, and both graduates of their respective institutions. Just free from the restraints of study, they enjoyed their present out-door life with all the frolicsome mirth of children. Daniel was away up at the lead-mines making his fortune; and these two, who had always been more sympathetic in their tastes, enjoyed each other's society exceedingly. On this particular day Mrs. Potter had charged them not to come home until the buckets they carried were brimful, for she wanted to make preserves.

The trees to which they directed their steps were two miles from the house, a little cluster out on the open prairie. Mrs. Potter had made preserves from those trees every fall for several years. As the young couple, in the highest of spirits, started off, their buckets on their arms, she had looked after them with admiration—they were truly a handsome pair, and she hardly knew which was dearest to her.

"Dear me, Peter, do you know I sometimes think she'll be our daughter in good earnest," she remarked, as she turned away. "The boys set a dreadful store by her, specially Amos; he was always her favorite."

"Stuff, Melissy, stuff! still, I must say, she could go a great ways, and not find a better husband, if I do say it myself. That boy's smart enough for two—and that's not the best of it —he's honorable and high-minded as the day is long. Thar's nothing mean about Amos."

"I'm proud of both our boys. Daniel's steddy, and good is any body can ask, husband. Still, he hain't that itching to know every thing that Amos has. Daniel's good-locking, too."

"So's Amos. But, law, what's the use of talkin'; she may marry an earl yet, and forgit she ever saw a log-cabin."

"It's not in Edith Lancaster to forgit her friends, Peter Potter. That silly old man hasn't made half so much of a fool of her as he's tried to. She's a republican out and out. And she knows as well as I do, thar's mighty small chance of her ever being called from here. Howsumever, she mayn't fancy Amos, nor he her, as for that matter. I *do* hope he'll find a wife that's suitable when he does make up his mind to get married."

"Mothers never think their sons' wives are good enough, when like as not they're a sight *too* good. Don't be too par-tickler, wife, if the boy ever does bring a pardner home. You're too good-natured a woman for that."

"Wall, I should call this borrowin' trouble for the future," laughed Mrs. Potter, returning to her work.

While this conversation was going on between their elders, the young couple was making their way to the plum-trees. It was a delicious afternoon: cool, but full of sunshine; brilliant and exhilarating. Gorgeous flowers bloomed afar on the prairie, tinting it with rich hues; the horizon wore the soft purple of September; the distant bluffs slept in an atmosphere of amethystine splendor; the sky overhead was deeply blue. They reached the cluster of plum-trees. The fruit, crimson and gold in color, hung thickly on the low trees. It was not a very arduous task to pile the buckets with their fragrant treasures, which glowed in a rich heap

"like balls of gold
Which had in blood been rolled."

When the plums were gathered, they felt the pleasant look mother Nature wore too much to return home immediately Sitting at the foot of a tree, whose shadows shimmered over them in the light breeze, they chatted about trifles, as the gay-hearted will, looking off over the level landscape with dreamy, blissful eyes. Amos had improved his four years, and they had improved him—deepening the hazel of his eyes and the brown of his hair, filling out his frame, and refining his looks and manners. If he had thought Edith marvelously lovely when he first met her, after their long absence, she also had thought how handsome he was, and how attractive his genial, pleasant ways. What else either of them had thought, perhaps, they were not themselves aware. But now the spell began to work. The impressive silence, the magnificent loveliness of the prairie, made them draw near to each other; and the brilliant sunshine, the splendid hues of vast spaces covered with flowers, infused them with glowing sentiment. They ceased to gossip about trifles, sinking into that silence which is more eloquent than words. The soft rustle of the leaves, and the still softer murmur of the tall prairie grass, were the sounds which made the silence more intense. Then there was another sound—Amos sighed, equal to any furnace, and Edith echoed his sigh. Then, beginning to feel vaguely conscious, she pulled off her straw hat, and began twisting leaves and flowers in the band. Somebody's fingers got tangled with hers in the ribbon; the hat fell down neglected.

"Edith !"

She looked up into the wistful eyes, and down again quickly Somebody's arm was around her waist, and somebody kissed her. And in the midst of her sweet confusion of blushes and smiles, somebody said something about love, and would somebody be his wife? Trying afterward to think it all over coolly, she remembered her emotions of fear and delight and surprise better than she did the precise words which had occasioned them. And then they sat, in the content of the fullest happiness, her head on his shoulder, and his arm about her waist, while the shadows shimmered over them, making the pretty picture still prettier.

Which brings us back to the beginning of this chapter.

For when it chanced that James Pipkin, trotting over the prairie after his lost cow, beheld the couple from afar, he groaned in anguish of spirit:

"O Lord, that ever I should 'ave come to a country like this !"

To see that son of a squatter, that child of a Peter Potter, that boy who used to wear his father's breeches made over, that Hamerican, that—that—himpertinent young rascal, with his arm around *his* young lady's waist, was hastonishing, himpudent, and hextraordinary.

His faith in the ultimate destiny of his darling had been as firm as a Christian's belief in his creed. That she would some time be claimed by her family, make a sensation with her beauty and her novel history, and be wooed and won by at ,cast a peer of the realm, had been the belief which had sustained him through all the perils and vicissitudes of seventeen long and lonely years. And now to see her ready to throw herself away upon this young clodhopper, just as soon as she was old enough to have a will of her own, was a stinging proof to him of the natural ingratitude of even the best of children. The clump of trees hid him from the view of the lovers, who were too much absorbed in themselves to think of any one else, or even to hear the faint footfalls of a traveler's steed, which was walking with grass and earth-muffled tread directly toward James and themselves. James' thin old blood had thickened up so hot and beat in his ears so, with anger and indignation, that he also did not hear the approach of the horse, till he was suddenly saluted, in Yankee nasal twang, with:

"Hello, old feller, what are you prancing about, like a mad hornet, for?"

Mr. Pipkin, turning suddenly, beheld a gaunt and raw-boned man upon a gaunt and raw-boned animal, over which his long legs dangled almost to the ground. His small, twinkling gray eyes, peaked nose, and the peculiar twist of his mouth, revealed at once a genius for prying into other people's affairs, sticking his nose into other people's business, and asking questions, *ad infinitum*. One cheek had a swollen appearance, in consequence of the enormous tobacco-quid within; he had on a striped cotton neck-tie, a calico shirt, a light-striped vest, a flowered blue-and-white coat, and a pair of plaid trowsers; his tow-colored head was shaded by a sombrero with an immense brim, and his feet were encased in boots, which—well, we'll hear his own story about them.

"Be you lookin' at them butes?" he continued, without waiting for an answer to his first question, as the little Englishman cast a hurried glance at him. "You needn't be surprised at their size. I had 'em made to carry my baggage in, to save the trouble of a valise, travelin' over the perrary. It's an uncommon convenient way of carrying your clo'es. Thar's a bull cowhide in each one—fact, stranger! come off my own cows, and I seen 'em made up. Jeminy! do you doubt me?"

"Not—not—in the least," stammered Mr. Pipkin, terrified at the length of the arm stretched suddenly out toward him.

"Don't be scart. I was just thinkin' I'd like to lift you, and give you a good shake, to see how heavy you was. Look as if the wing of a muskeeter might blow you away? Was you ever weighed?"

"Not lately."

"What in the name of all that's funny do you wear your hair tied up in that tail for? Say, old feller?"

"All of the Lancaster family servants wear their 'air in a cue," said James, beginning to put on the dignity out of which he had been frightened.

"Oh, they du, du they? And who be the Lancasters? No great shakes, I'll bet a dog's tail."

"They're one of the holdest and richest families in Heng-land, sir. If you wasn't as hignorant as Hamericans generally, you wouldn't 'ave to inquire."

"English, be you? I thought as much. You look like a little, squeaking, vain-glorious rat from t'other side the water. Jeminy! whew! but didn't we lick you well, a spell ago? But of course you can't remember no sich onpleasant fact as that. Say, now, you haven't answered my question yet—what was you raring and tearing round so about?"

"Do you see that couple of young people under those plum-trees?"

"To be sure I do. I seen 'em long ago. I seen em' kiss-ing and hugging and having a tol'able good time; and I seen 'em jump as if they was shot, when I hollered eout to you a a minit ago."

"That's just what I'm so hindignant about, sir. To think that a Lancaster would up and haccept for a lover that him-pertinent youngster—that low-bred Hamerican—that 'oosier, sir."

"Oh, ho! *that's* it, is it? Is the young lady your daughter, sir?"

"She's the daughter of a Lancaster, and I be nothing but her servant. 'Er father confided her to my charge, and I shall be heternally disgraced if she marries that scoundrel. Why, he's a Potter! Just think of it—a Potter! O Lord, it's worse than a Pipkin!"

"A Potter? you don't say so! Then I'm on the right track. He's the son of my old friend Peter, I reckon. Can you tell me how fur it is to their place? Jeminy! but that's a handsome girl! I'll swear I don't blame the feller. He'd be a fool if he didn't make love to her."

"I've lavished money on her, like water," grumbled the old man. "I've waited on her all her life. Sixteen bushels of carrots and twenty bushels of parsnips and honions, sixteen bushels of beets and a 'undred bushels of potatoes did I raise with my own old 'ands, and sell to pay her last term. I've set out strawberry beds, and bent hover them till my back ached like the toothache, a-purpose to buy her a pianny this fall. It's enough to kill me to see her a-going so. O Lord, that ever she should 'ave growed up in a country like this!"

"Look-a-here, stranger, this is a fust-rate country, and don't you never insinuate nothing to the contrary in *my* presence. I'm mighty partickler what's said about Uncle Sam, and when I'm riled, I'm a terrible feller. My knuckles are all hard and horny, jist with the men I've knocked down, that was so impudent as to rile me. Look at 'em, now?"

"I beg your pardon, sir. I meant no disrespect to Hamerica, which is a very fine place to those as be used to it," spoke the little man, drawing away from the vicinity of the huge fist. "But Miss Edith shall never be a Potter, for all that!" and as he whispered this last, he set his teeth together, as if he clenched a purpose with all the tenacity of a little old gray terrier shaking some poor mouse to pieces.

"Hello, you there! don't be hurrying away so fast," shouted the stranger, to the lovers, who had taken up their buckets for a start; and kicking his horse with his heel, he rode up beside them.

"You're a Potter, sure enough," he said, after a keen survey of Amos. "You're your fayther over again, only a little more finnified. Say, young man, did you ever hecr your fayther speak of his old friend, 'Zekiel Purson?"

"Indeed, I have," answered Amos, heartily; "are you Mr Purson?"

"Don't mister me, if you please. Call me Uncle 'Zeke. I should have been your uncle if Prudence Potter hadn't given me the mitten, eout and eout. Say, you puss, you don't intend to serve anybody you know as bad a trick as that, do you?"

Edith's blushing smile had hardly answered him before James had hurried up, gasping for breath, and seized her arm.

"Come right straight home, my dear young lady, if you please."

"What will I do with the plums, James?"

"Oh, I'll take the plums up here," answered the ready Yankee. "You go along home, and take that old feller's scolding for behaving as a young woman ought to. You'll get the better of him, *I'll* bet. Come over to-morrow, and tell us all about it; for I reckon I shall stop a spell at Peter Potter's."

Amos was disappointed at this abrupt termination to their tête-à-tête, but it was a small disappointment to others which were to follow in its wake.

CHAPTER V.

THE RECOGNIZED PORTRAIT.

A LADY and gentleman, in the prime of life, were walking leisurely from picture to picture in the London Royal Academy, when both, as by one impulse, started and paused before the " Portrait of a Lady."

" It is Edith herself !" muttered the gentleman.

" It is certainly marvelously like her," said his companion. " I did not know there were any portraits of her, except the one we have in our chamber."

This was said in a voice of habitual softness, and the elegant·woman gave no sign of uneasiness, except by pretending to arrange, for an instant, the folds of her mantle. ·Perhaps she felt no uneasiness as yet, except that vague fear which never ceases entirely to haunt those who have been guilty of an undetected crime.

A young artist, standing near with a group of his fellows, drew closer as he observed their interest, scanning them with as keen a gaze as they the picture.

" It is Edith, and yet it is not her," continued the gentleman ; " I see myself in that face, also—I am sure of it, Margaret. Do not you see a resemblance, or is it my imagination ?"

" It is your imagination, I think, Edwin. Constant dreaming over any great loss or sorrow, will not only disease the mind but the eye. O Edwin ! why can not your Margaret win you from the past ?"

Her voice sank to a tender whisper, and her dark eyes filled with tears, which gave a sudden charm to her cold and haughty features. The artist regarded them both attentively. He had a clue to the innermost meaning of their conversation ; *he* saw the likeness which the lady denied, and he saw, also, something in the beautiful face of that woman which the husband by her side, during the long years of his life with her, had never detected—a capability of evil ; or, perhaps, rather a firmness of selfishness which would not swerve from its purpose to save any more yielding object which might be in its way. Almost instantaneously his mind sprang to a conclusion, vague in detail but distinct in form.

"Did you inquire if this were a portrait or an ideal face ?" he asked, pretending to have understood such a question from the visitors

The gentleman turned to him eagerly.

"Did you paint it ?"

"I did—and from the life. I can show you the first sketch here in my portfolio. Would you like to see it ?"

He opened the portfolio, and drew out the sketch. The strangers looked at it earnestly.

"Edith !—was that her name ?" asked the gentleman, seeing it written under the likeness.

"Her name was Edith. Do you see any thing else written upon the corner of the sheet ?"

"Illinois prairie, Beaver Creek, May 18—," continued the gentleman. "Well, sir, tell me all about it, quickly," he continued, almost sternly, in his impatience and suspense.

"I have no objections to telling you all you desire to know," answered the young artist, a little indifferently, looking as closely at the agitated faces before him as if he had not painted this picture with the hope that it might some time produce such a scene. "Last spring and summer I was traveling on a sketching-tour, through the United States, when I—"

"The United States !"

"When I chanced upon a bit of prairie-scenery, so very lovely that I staid over night at a friendly farm-house to complete my sketch. The farmer who entertained me, and whose name was Potter—"

"Potter !" again burst forth from the gentleman's lips.

"Was very hospitable. After I left his house, in the morning, and was busy with my sketch again, the original of this portrait appeared suddenly in the landscape, and being occupied like myself, sat very quietly while I joyfully added her to my paper. It's a sweet young face, don't you think so ? I had the pleasure of being introduced to her, shortly afterward, at the farmer's dinner-table. I learned that she was of English parentage, and that her name was Lancaster."

"Great Heaven, Margaret, it is my child!"

The artist looked at the lady—she was very pale, and her eye drooped beneath his glance. At that moment a fine-looking boy of fifteen came into the hall, and approached them.

"Here I am, mamma, just in time!" he exclaimed.

In the look of pride and love, now mingled with something dark and bitter, which the lady turned upon the handsome boy, the artist read the secret of her chagrin at the appearance of an older child.

"Was she well? Was she happy? Who did she live with—how?"

"If she's grown up in a log-cabin, I'm afraid you won't be very much pleased with her, Edwin," half-laughed the lady, before the artist could answer her husband's hurried inquiries.

But again her eyes quailed before the searching look of the stranger who had given them this unlooked-for information, and who now said impressively:

"Allow me, madam, to disabuse your mind of any such fear. I never saw a more beautiful young lady than Miss Edith Lancaster; and, although her faithful friend and servant, James Pipkin, gardener and farmer, seemed afflicted with the same apprehension as yourself of the fatal result of contact with pig-pens and dirt-pies, I must say, that for gentle breeding, as well as natural grace, Miss Edith is quite peerless."

There was a touch of impertinence in the manner of the artist, for he mistrusted the lady and did not like her demeanor, but Mr. Lancaster was obliged to overlook this in the necessity for getting farther information from the only person who could give it. He begged Mr. Beverly to go with him to his own house, where they could be more retired, and there tell him every circumstance of this chance-meeting with his long-lost daughter. The party descended to his carriage, and were driven to the town-house of the Lancasters, where, in the privacy of the library, the artist related the story, to the minutest particular—the occupations of James; the confidence of the old man who had shown him the portraits, jewels, etc. in his possession; every look and word of the young girl, that she was well, and happy, and a most lovely, lovable creature; and that he had placed her picture in the academy in the hope that it might lead to some discovery beneficial to her.

"And now," said he, in conclusion, "I think it will not be out of place for me to inquire, in return, what train of circumstances could have kept you in ignorance of her existence, when James did not cease to write to you for years."

"There has been foul play somewhere," was the answer. "I did receive a letter from James, stating that the babe was dead, and that the inducements to remain in America were so strong, that he should not return until he had made a fortune. I smiled at the little fellow's ambition, and have always expected that he would some day get homesick and return to us."

"Of course that letter was a forgery," remarked Mr. Beverly.

"It must have been—but whose?—and for what purpose?" mused Mr. Lancaster.

His wife, who had been sitting by his side, but where he could not see her face, now excused herself to the stranger, and retired from the room on the plea of a headache.

Shortly after Mr. Beverly departed, with the warm thanks of the gentleman of the house, and a commission for a couple of pictures.

Whatever suspicions Mr. Lancaster had failed to express before his visitor, continued to deepen in his mind until they became irresistible. He sought the chamber of his wife, and his sharp gaze did not fail to detect her changing color, which she hoped to have passed as the effects of a violent headache. After looking at her, for what seemed to her an age, he remarked:

"You know something of this matter, Margaret."

"I do—it was I who forged that letter!"

She burst into tears as she made this avowal, drawn from her unexpectedly by the conviction expressed in his manner.

"*You*, Margaret! and with what motive?"

His accent of surprise and scorn stung her to the heart; her head sank lower and her tears flowed faster. It was the first time Mr. Lancaster had ever seen his haughty and brilliant wife humiliated by any circumstances. He was standing by her side, as she sat in the arm-chair, where she had thrown herself on pretense of illness. Suddenly she looked up with a passionate glance, through her tears, caught his hand and held it tightly:

"I could bear no more rivals in your love, Edwin."

The consummate tact of this answer was made apparent by the softening of the stern eyes fixed upon her. Yet the reply was the true one.

Margaret, when a girl, before his first marriage, had loved Edwin Lancaster; she had tried to conquer him, as she had conquered so many others, for she was exceedingly beautiful, tasteful in dress, brilliant in manners; a belle by beauty and position, for her family was excellent, and she was the heiress of a large property. When the only man she really favored, out of all with whom she had coquetted, ran away with a minister's dowerless daughter, her chagrin and disappointment were both great.

She had not yet found another so much to her liking when ne returned, a widower, more captivating to her than before; she resolved to win him, and she succeeded.

Margaret's was not simply one of those cold and selfish natures which delights in triumphs and artifices; she was subtle and haughty, but she was passionately devoted to the few whom she honored with her love. It was not often that she stooped to absolute deceit; nor was she hardy enough to venture upon a really criminal thing, yet she had a lack of that nobility of soul which will die before it will yield to temptation—a great temptation was thrown in her way, and she yielded.

She was visiting Mr. Lancaster's sister, shortly after his return home. She had always maintained a friendship with Blanche Lancaster, which she now made available for a long visit to their country-house, where, day by day, she had opportunities of insinuating a little sunshine into the darkness of the young widower's mourning. Touched by her gentle interest, he had more than once allowed himself to dwell upon his grief, had spoken to her of the babe he had been obliged to leave behind him, and of the tie it was, binding him to hopes which, otherwise, would be despairs.

An intense jealousy of this hope and this tie made her miserable. Certain as she was that, sooner or later, she should become his wife, she did not like the prospect of being stepmother to a little girl whose probable resemblance to the first wife would be a constant reminder of the past.

One morning she was in the breakfast-room, when a footman brought in the letters; neither Blanche nor Edwin had descended from their chambers; there were letters for all, and with the package which the senior Mr. Lancaster handed her, by mistake was one for Edwin. It was post-marked United States. She knew that he was looking anxiously for news—what evil genius prompted her to slip that letter into her pocket, and say nothing of the mistake? After breakfast, she locked herself in her chamber, and, after a half-hour's desperate struggle with her conscience, she broke the seal, and read old James's crooked and curious chirography, from which she deciphered the well-being of the infant, and the anxiety of the servant to return home as soon as possible. Carefully preserving the envelope, which she had opened with skill, she labored until she could imitate the writing of the servant; when she wrote another and quite different epistle, containing news of the babe's death, and the servant's desire to remain where he was; this she inclosed in the same envelope, and burning all traces of her work, she managed, at the arrival of the next mail, to drop the letter beside of Mr. Lancaster, who soon perceived it, and thinking himself had let it fall, gathered it up and gave it to his son.

Thus the first step was taken; but it was not the last. Margaret hardened herself to the grief of the young father, listened prettily to his regrets that he had left the child, condoled with him, sympathized, comforted him. But she acted without sufficient reflection. How was she to arrest the course of future letters which would undo all she had done? In her perplexity she bitterly regretted the foolish selfishness which had urged her to such needless and uncomfortable folly. She would have welcomed the child, if its appearance could have relieved her of the effects of that one guilty step. The dread of betrayal haunted her. It was by incredible painstaking and plotting that she intercepted and destroyed the next two letters; and, in the mean time, her wooing—for she did her wooing in her charming way—went on slowly. If she had been in haste, from love, to be the wife of the man she adored, she was now doubly in haste from fear.

So it happened that Edwin Lancaster, like many other grieving husbands, was the bridegroom of another beautiful lady, before the second anniversary of the death of that fair flower he had transplanted to a new world only to perish.

After she had achieved the object of her life, Margaret had no longer much trouble in keeping up the deception. She had a habit of receiving and opening the budget of letters herself, that she might intercept any stray missive which occasionally straggled along from America. This habit Mr. Lancaster attributed to the kindness and industry of his brilliant wife, who frequently lent him her aid, in the hurry of business, acting as his private secretary. He had always respected and admired, rather than loved her. She had won him by a determination to do so; and he had been proud of her, though his heart, in its gentlest and tenderest depths, was consecrated to a memory. This Margaret was aware of; and that exclusiveness of possession, that jealousy, which was one of her leading characteristics, embittered the knowledge to her. Their boy, so bright and handsome, was the idol of his father; she smiled to see it, and felt more and more as if she could not allow that unknown older child to come in and divide that love.

Yet the shadow of her guilt possessed her; she often felt like one who walks upon ice. Finally the passage of seventeen years had almost obliterated her fears; the matter became to her as if it were not. Then, right in the midst of her security, came her betrayal. Humble and guilty she wept before her husband, making her great love the excuse for her wrong-doing.

CHAPTER VI.

NEWS FROM THE "HOLD" COUNTRY.

" SAY, yeou, what you sittin' thar under that tree fer, with two tears drippin' down your cheeks like rain down a couple oi pink hollyhocks ?"

Edith started as the voice of Uncle Zeke met her ears. It was the day after his sudden appearance on the prairie, and she had not seen her lover since. Something which James had said had cast down her spirits so much, that she had stolen out into the apple-orchard to have a good cry. Mr. Purson had come over to make a friendly and inquisitive call on his English acquaintance of yesterday, and also to be the bearer of an invitation to Miss Edith, which Amos was too busy to deliver in person.

" You'll look purty at the party to-night, if you go and sile up them shiny eyes in that style. Come! come! quit off, now, and give 'em time to settle."

" What party ?" queried the young lady, smiling at her odd visitor, in spite of the unutterable misery which afflicted her.

" Why, the huskin'-bee, to be sure. I told my friend Peter, this mornin', I'd like some kind of a jolly time, as I couldn't stay long, and he suddenly found out the corn had got to be husked, and by flyin' round they could git ready for the bee to-night. So Amos's gone to town to git some of the fixin's, and ask the young folks out, and his mother's bakin' cake like smash—you can smell it a quarter of a mile from the house— and stewin' plums and apple-sass, and cookin' pies. I picked seventeen fowls for her, 'fore I come over here. So now, Miss Lancaster, I came to ask you if you'd be so perlite as to do me the favor of accepting my escort to the huskin'-bee ? I can't promise to bring you hum, but I've got a nephew as will see to that. Don't give me the mitten now, don't !"

" I have no intention of treating you so cruelly," replied Edith, the sun breaking through the clouds of her trouble.

" Thank you. I shall certingly have the honor of the com·

pany of the purtiest girl at the frolic.   Only about them tears!
—you hain't told me what you was cryin' about yet."

"Oh, never mind, Mr. Purson, what it was."

"I just want to satisfy myself if it was about any thing *I'm*
concerned in.   Has that little imp of a blue-tailed-coat feller
been a putting on airs to yeou, and a tellin' yeou, yeou must
mind *him?*"

"Don't speak so, please, Mr. Purson; he's so good, so kind,
I love him so much—only—only he don't think so much of
Amos as I do; and he says he's going to take me to Eng-
land, this very month, whether I want to go or not."

"He duz, duz he?   He'd better ask my nephew what he
thinks about it, first.   I guess you'll go when Amos gets
ready to let you."

"Oh, but I can not endure to forsake him entirely, after
he's devoted his very life to me for so long; and he says *he*
shall go, whether I do or not.   When he goes, I shall be left
entirely unprotected and unprovided for, if I refuse—"

"Guess Amos'll take care of that,"

"But I don't want him to—not so soon—we're so young,
you know,"—and she blushed; "and it would be so ungrateful of me to let poor, dear, good old James go alone."

"I guess he's old enough to go alone.   If he wants to make
a fool of himself, and go trotting off to England to find folks
that don't care a copper about you, let him go.   There's folks
here as *does* care about you.   And if he makes *yeou* any trou
ble, I'll shake him to pieces."

"Oh no, you will do nothing of the kind," laughed Edith,
as he made this threat with a ferocious air, not very frightful
after all.   "I shouldn't allow it."

"Shouldn't, hey?   Waal, just tell me where to find him,
and I'll have a little sociable talk with him, while you're git-
ting ready for the party; for Mrs. Potter wants you to come
right over now, and give her your advice about caraway seeds
in the gingerbread, and sugar in the punkin'-pies, to say
nothin' of settin' the table—whether it shall be sot bottom-side
up or top-side down, on this important occasion."

"You'll find James attending to his dahlias in front of the
house; I shall not be long getting ready," and she flitted into
the house to prepare for the husking-bee.

Mr. Ezekiel Purson made his way to the flower-garden, to beguile the short period of his stay with conversation—an occupation of which he was particularly fond.

"Waal, Mr. Pipkin, how are ye to-day ? Got reconciled to the match ?"

"What match, sir ?" asked James, laying down the wisp of straw he was binding about a young shrub, and standing as stiffly as if he had suddenly been converted into a post.

"Oh, none in pertickler—a brimstun' match, I reckon—leastwise, it's sure to go off. Puttin' overcoats on your flowers, are ye ?"

"They need overcoats to stand these 'ere western winters, sir. This is a hawful climate. In the summer the thermometer almost runs over, and in the winter it's way down to zero."

"Down to zero ! thunderation ! you've no idea what it is in Vermont. I've known it to run way down into the bulb, and then git so mad 'cause it couldn't go any further, it would freeze up and bust its biler. In July and August it *always* steams—fact, Mr. Pipkin ! But as for you saying it ain't an agreeable climate, that's all a mistake. It ain't healthy for people that don't like it, and I shouldn't wonder if it killed *you* 'fore you was a hundred years older. Say, now, how old be you ? I'm reckoned to be pretty cute at guessing, but I couldn't guess within a hundred and fifty years of your right age, now."

"An 'undred and fifty years, Mr. Purson !"

"Yes, *sir !* Why, when I first seen you, out on the perrarie, kicking up the grass and tearin' round so, I thought it was old Methusalah himself. But come to see you a second time, you look younger. I should say you weren't more'n three or four centuries old; but, come ! I wish you'd let a feller know *per*cisely."

"I shall be sixty-two come January."

"Git eout ! is that all ? Yeou don't look as if yeou'd last much longer, and it would be a great pity fer yeou to be taken off the hooks, and leave that purty girl of your'n without nobody to see to her. Better see her safely married to some likely young feller."

"I intend to," was the curt reply.

" Du ycou, r'ally ? My nephew 'll be tickled to death to hear that. He's orfully smitten."

" It won't be to any farmer's son, nor nobody else she'll be likely to meet in this country."

" 'Twon't, hey ? Maybe you think she'll catch the President, if she ever gits a chance. He's only a trifle older than you be, and a fine old bachelor, humly as a mud fence."

" I wouldn't stay here any longer, if I knew she'd catch a President ; I'm going 'ome and going to take her along."

. " Tell you what it is, friend, if you want to live a good long life, you'd better stay in this country. Git your darter—"

" She isn't my daughter."

" Git your young lady safely married to my ncphew, and then sell out here, and go back with me to Vermont. In the part of the State where I live people seldom dies. After they get to be so old nobody remembers when they was born or who they are, they begin to dry up, and in the course of seventy or eighty years after that, they've become about the size of children ; and then they go up into the mountains and disappear."

" Disappear ?"

" Yes, entirely—don't even leave any bones. It's always been a mystery what becomes of 'em—it's reckoned a special dispensation of Providence takes 'em off somehow, to git rid of 'em. Howsumever, though you might live to a good old age by 'migrating to Vermont, you wouldn't find the land quite so good for your business as this. Boulders are so thick thar the sheep have to have their noses sharpened on grin'-stuns before they can git at the grass—fact, friend. Have you ever had any fights with the snakes since you settled in these parts ? Massasowgers thick about here, ain't they ? Last week as I was walking through the big woods to the north ot here about fifty mile, I saw suthin' a rolling along that looked like a hoop to a nail-keg. ' Jehosaphat !' says I to myself, ' what on airth makes that hoop trundle along without anybody's help ?' and I hadn't any more'n got the thought into my mind, then I recollected what I'd been told about a certain kind of snake, called a hoop snake, that rolled after that fashion, and struck with its tail, and that it was deadly pisen—at least twice as pisenous as the rattlesnake. By the time I'd come to this conclusion 'twan't ten feet from me; 'twan't no use to run, for, though Zeke Purson's got purty long legs, they wouldn't stand any chance at all against travel-in' by wheel, as that feller traveled. Well, sir, I didn't have time to *think* what to do, but I done it by instinct,—jist as he'd got about one more turn to make, I gave a rousing jump and jumped clear over him. By the time he'd picked him-self up and looked around, I was ready to spring back again, —and thar we had it, backards and foreards for at least an hour. It's a pecooliarity of the hoop-snake that it can't turn without some trouble, though it can run like lightnin'. My only chance was to tire him out, and finally, whether he got tired, or felt ashamed of himself, or was too much astonished at the look of things to keep on tryin', I can't say, but he jist wheeled about and rolled off in another direction as fast as his fatigue would allow him. It's a wonder he didn't bite himself he got so all-fired mad. Wa'll! I was a little used up myself,—felt as if the hinges of my back wanted 'ilen,—and I felt relieved—sakes! thar's Miss Edith all ready for me to beau her over to my friend Potter's. You've been as spry as a kitten, sis; you look as rosy as a spitzenberg, and as sweet as taffy. Cracky! but don't I envy Amos Potter! I wish I was as young as he, and thrash me if I wouldn't try to cut him out. You needn't feel troubled about your young lady if she don't get home very early; she's goin' to a corn-huskin' and she's under my protection. She'll be as safe under my pro-tection, as the goddess of liberty is under the shadder of the great spread eagle. Don't you believe it, Miss Edith?"

The young girl laughed, despite of James's cross looks; she put her arms about the old servant's neck and kissed him good-by in a way that threw her escort into despair.

"Yeour a lucky man, Mr. Pipkin. I wish somebody 'd do that to me. I could afford to let 'em go to a huskin'-bee. Are you ready, Miss Edith? 'spect Mrs. Potter will be in as much of a stew as her plum preserves if we don't git along purty soon. Speakin' of plum preserves, puts me in mind to ask you if you'r fond of going a plum-hunting on the perraries, Miss Lancaster?"

Edith, who had a vivid remembrance of some occurrences which had been observed under the plum-trees the previous day, was glad to run forward and open the gate into the road, as an excuse for hiding her embarrassment.

"Allow me to do the perlite after this," said Mr. Purson, with an excruciating bow, springing after her in time to close the gate, and offering her the "crook of his elbow," which she declined, it being too far above her to be of essential service; besides the necessity she would be under of taking at least two steps to his one.

"I'm glad you come right over," said Mrs. Potter, as Edith appeared at the door with her companion. "Amos hasn't got back from the village yet, but I'm expectin' him every minit! He's in real good spirits and likes the idea of the frolic amazingly. He's bound to get a fiddler, and finish off with a dance. Let's see! you used to be suthin' of a dancer, didn't. you, Mr. Purson?"

"*Used* to be, Millissa! I reckon I'm some at it, yet. Give me a purty girl, and a good fiddler, and I'll out-dance the spryest feller at the bee to-night. Say, Miss Edith, I want to speak about that matter, now, 'fore Amos gets back. You're promised to me for the first set—mind! I shall pick a quarrel with any other beau you dare to dance with."

"I'll consider myself engaged to you, Mr. Purson."

"Amos will be mad as pop-corn when he finds it out. Wa'll, Mellissa, we're ready for work, both of us. Any more fowls to pick, or spice to grind, or kindlin'-wood to split, or ovens to clear out?—if there ain't, I'll go to the barn and see how Peter's gettin' it fixed. That barn-floor will be a grand place to dance; the threshin'-floor is extra smooth, I noticed, and plenty of room for full swing."

Finding Mrs. Potter had no more "chorcs" for him at present, he left them to search out friend Peter, who was getting the barn swept clean and the corn in a great pile on the floor.

Edith tied on one of Mrs. Potter's big check aprons over her pretty dress and was ready to assist, but was not allowed to soil her hands with any thing serious to perform. She had studied James' cook book to some purpose, for she made some delectable "cup" and "delicate" cake,—her friend's knowledge not extending beyond gingerbread, doughnuts, and cookies. She was beating up the frosting for this cake, which was nearly ready to come out of the oven, her face brilliant with excitement and exercise, when a shadow darkened the sunshine streaming in at the open door. She knew that Amos stood there, looking at her, but she dared not raise her eyes. That sweet confusion which fills a maiden's heart the first time she meets her lover, after he has won her confession of interest in him, sent waves of color flushing over her cheeks; she was afraid he would notice how loudly her pulse throbbed. He stood there so long silent, enjoying her blushes, that his mother, who had been absent in the "front-room," dusting the furniture, was heard returning to the kitchen, which made Edith raise her eyes, and thus discover that there was trouble as well as joy mingled in the expression of her lover's face.

"Couldn't you get a fiddler?" asked Mrs. Potter.

"Oh yes, mother—all right. The girls and boys are coming, the nuts and raisins and lump-sugar are in the basket; and the fiddler is glad of a chance of playing for a husking-bee."

"I thought you looked kind of disappointed," said the mother.

He made no reply just then; but after he had brought the basket in, and unloaded the brick-oven of its freight of pies and cakes, he approached Edith and said in an undertone-

"I brought James a letter, as I came along."

His manner startled her, even before she had time to think of what consequence that simple fact might be to her.

"Where from?"

"England. The old man is wild with joy. He begged of me to stop and read it to him, I could make it out so much more quickly than he. He jumped up and down with glee, to the ruin of his dahlia-bulbs."

"Who was it from?"

"Your father. Don't tremble so, Edith. He writes that he has just learned of your being in existence, and will come for you by the next steamer!"

"O, Amos!"

"James wanted you to come home immediately, to talk over the news. Of course you will go, Edith. The frolic is ruined for me."

"I will go; but it is only a mile and back. I shall be here again before the huskers get to work. It's four o'clock now, and I suppose you don't expect them before six."

"I wish I could be your companion; but it would be unfair to desert mother in the midst of her emergencies. I've two quarts of coffee to grind, and innumerable odds and ends to straighten out; and there's the final touches to be given. Don't fail to return, Edith, if you want me to dance any."

"I shall return," answered the young girl, as she threw on her sun-bonnet and hurried away, her heart beating faster with conflicting emotions than it had ever beat before.

Had she heard this news, even a week sooner, it would not have affected her as deeply as it did now. It seemed to send her being into two conflicting tides—the joy, wonder, and expectation which she might have felt rising up only to meet the surging waves of her newly avowed love. Her father was coming—but he was coming to take her away. If James' prejudices against the young American were so strong, would not her father share in those prejudices? would she not be called upon to make a choice between old friends and new, instead of having the double happiness of belonging to both!

Yet it might not be so. Her father was a gentleman; he would recognize those noble qualities in Amos Potter which the ignorance of the narrow-minded servant would not permit him to do. Surely he would not annul his boundless obligations to the Potters, by setting a barrier between his child and their's. No, no! her father would respect, advise, and sometime love the young man, the plainness of whose family was his only fault.

While Edith sped along, full of these fears and hopes, Amos went on with his preparations for the frolic with rather a doleful face. He seemed to be grinding the coffee to the tune of "The Crying Family." He was a modest, although a self-respecting youth, and all his faith was not sufficient to convince him that his merits were powerful enough to overcome the superior temptations of riches, novelty, foreign travel, a home of splendor, and a proud father. That happy day which had danced before his imagination with a bewildering nearness and brightness, that day of days when he should take unto himself a wife—of which he had dreamed constantly for the last thirty-six hours—seemed to flee and fade into the far future, growing so dim, shadowy, and uncertain that it was no better than a mocking phantom.

"Hello! what's the matter? Got the toothache?" exclaimed Zeke, returning from the barn. "How any feller can keep up a fit of the blues and smell them turkeys roasting, beats me. Thunderation! where's that streak of sunshine gone to, that was shinin' round here a spell ago? Don't wonder the place looks gloomy. What's that? She's gone home to read her father's letter, who's coming in the next steamer to carry her off? Whew! that explains the toothache, does it? Scissors and knives! that'll never do—*never!* You don't intend to submit to it, do you, my boy?"

"If she wishes to go, I can not help it, can I, Uncle Zeke?"

"But she *won't* want to go, if you tease her not to—which you'll be a thunderin' fool if you don't do. Didn't I catch her cryin' her eyes out at the idea, this very afternoon? If I had a grl head over ears in love with *me*, guess I shouldn't let nothing interfere between us. It's as plain to be seen that she's orfully smitten with you, as the hands on the face of that clock. Speaking of clocks, I've got a load over to Wakwaka and if you think it'd be a good specilation to bring 'em to Beaver Creek, I'll do it, next week."

"*We* want a new clock, dreadfully," said Mrs. Potter, who, in bustling from one room to another, came in, in time to hear these last remarks. "Our'n is all out of order—one of the hands is broke, and it loses an hour every day. It's likely a good part of the neighbors would take a clock, if you have 'em cheaper than they do to Beaver Creek."

"Cheaper! I guess I have! Cheaper and better, by a long sight. I've got clocks that go like greased lightnin', that I sell for a dolla' an' fifty cents—purty clocks too, mahogany frames and lookin'-glasses sot in 'em—you get a time-piece for twelve shillin's and a mirror thrown in. I'm glad *you* want a clock, Mellissa,—I shall take unexpressible pleasure in conferring the best of the lot upon you, as soon as they arrive!"

"Oh, thank you Zekiel. Bless me! if thar' ain't the Sampsons comin' a'ready. You run out, Amos, and see 'em in, while I go up stair and slip on another dress. I'se afraid I'd be late."

It did not take Mrs. Potter many moments to reappear from her chamber, with a neat gingham dress and black silk apron on; which she considered good enough for the occasion, considering the work there was on hand. Three bouncing girls and two stout, awkward boys, all very good to work and equally good to dance and enjoy themselves after it, were the representatives of the Sampson family, whom the hostess welcomed in the front room, where the girls had already taken off their bonnets. From this time on, for the next hour, there was a steady flow of arrivals; mostly of farmers' sons and daughters, who knew just what a corn-husking meant, and came to be useful; there were also a few from the village, who wore finer clothes than was proper for the occasion, who didn't know how to husk corn, and who came only for the amusement. However, Amos had used the good-sense in giving in invitations, not to invite any of his more polished friends who would "put on airs" and offend their country cousins; so that those who came from the village, although erring from ignorance, made good-natured attempts to assimilate themselves to those about them; and, by sunset, a large and merry company were seated in a circle upor the barn-floor, in the center of which was heaped the unhusked corn.

Amos could hardly attend rightly to his work, nor keep up his side of the gay conversation with a pretty girl seated next him—one of Edith's friends from the seminary, who was amused and delighted with the idea of a genuine husking-bee —for his eyes were constantly wandering to the door. His anxiety was relieved at dusk by Edith slipping in and taking her place on the other side, welcomed joyfully by all who knew her.

Uncle Zeke had been introduced generally to the whole assembly, and particularly to the most of them. He was in high spirits, and whenever the flashing of his blue-and-white coat-tails and plaid trousers was discernible, those screams from the girls and roars of laughter from the young men attested to his success in making himself popular.

By the aid of a couple of dozen of the housewives' oldest and hardest-bleached tallow-candles, the barn was now bravely illuminated.

"Come, Uncle Zeke, aren't you going to perform your share of the work?' asked Amos, laughingly, seeing that he did not settle himself, but was buzzing about lke a great bumble-bee.

"Presently, presently, I'll pick out a purty girl for my pardner, and husk a bushel of corn with her on a wager. But business before pleasure, ladies and gentlemen ! When both can be combined, as on this occasion, it's better still. Now, when my old friend Peter made this frolic for me, he'd no idea I'd turn it to such good account. The fact is, I'm not only mighty fond of a party, but I consider it no harm to do a good stroke of bisness at the same time. I confer a benefit upon this community as well as upon myself, when I inform it that I'm engaged, at present, in sellin' patent rights. Now, Potter, if you'll excuse me for takin' up the 'tention of this company fer about ten minits, I'll explain myself. Are any of the fair bein's I behold around me in the habit of making butter ? You be ?—of course you be !—this is a fine dairy country. Very well. You spend from half an hour to a nour, a nour and a half, or two hours a churning every day, making your wrists ache, and spoiling your lovely tempers at the provoking, plaguey butter that's 'so long a-comin !' Wall, I've got a churn—I call it the ' MAGIC, GRAND-ACTION, SELF-REVOLVING, TWO-FORTY CHURN.' It's a pity I hadn't one here to show you to-night—shall have day after to-morror—but here's the model; you see how it goes off of itself. Wall, my fair countrywimming, that churn never fails to bring butter out of the poorest milk—mind, I say *milk*—don't even have to wait for the cream to raise—that churn brings butter in less 'n two minits and a half! Fact, my friends ! that's the reason why I call it the ' TWO-FORTY CHURN.' I don't sell the churns ready made ; but I want to sell the right to manefactor them to some enterprizing young man in this community, who'll be sure to make his everlastin' fortin' out of 'em, and consequently be able to marry any girl he wants. They go off like hot cakes. No farmer's wife or daughter who's ever seen one in operation, will give the old man a minit's peace till he's supplied her with one. It makes a third more butter out of the same quantity of milk in a space of time 'tain't worth mentioning. I'd almost said it salted it and worked it over, made it into pound pats, and carried it to market ; but, as I confine myself to the *strictest* truth, I shan't say so. All I will say is, it's a magic churn—the very witches is in it—cheap as a common one, almost, and will save my fair countrywimming money enough every year to buy themselves a silk frock, and time enough to wear it out.   And now you all want to buy it, and all are going to buy it; all that's wanting is for some fine feller to give me fifty dollars for the right for this county, and go to makin' 'em just as fast as he can make 'em."

"Maybe I'd buy it, if I had the fifty dollars," said a long-haired youth; "but I can't, for the same reason that I can't git married, though I want to most outrageously—I'm too poor."

"Poor! with that nice little black-eyed girl a sittin' by your side and blushin' like a piny. I'd consider myself as rich as gold if I'd a girl a lookin' like that at me.   If you hain't got fifty dollars, borrer it—borrer it, I say! you can pay it back in less 'n two weeks, and by the time them black eyes has got the weddin'-dress made up, you'll be able to git married and set up housekeepin' on your own hook.   You needn't larf, ladies and gentlemen, he can do it as slick as grease!"

"And I will do it, by hokey, shan't I, Sall?" muttered the young man, over whose lank countenance beamed an unwonted look of happiness which was reflected from the black eyes with double brilliancy: the "MAGIC, GRAND-ACTION, SELF-REVOLVING, TWO-FORTY CHURN" had already fulfilled a portion of its glorious mission by making two young people full of hope and anticipation.

"Waal, now, ladies and gentlemen, having blessed the female sect of this country in general, and this young lady in particular, and made the fortin' of this likely chap, at an expense so small that I'm almost ashamed to say it's only fifty dollars I've asked, I will, by the permission of friend Potter, introduce another idea to your consideration which has the welfare of the brothers and husbands of the wimmen more particularly in view.   I don't want you to think me a wicked person, bound on ruining an innocent and confiding community, when I tell you one of my objects is to disseminate a new *vice*,—yet such is the fact.   I reckon the ladies think the male sect has vices enough, and so it has; but they ain't of the right kind!   Here's the model of a vice, now, any farmer can make for himself in an hour's time, that'll hold on tighter than a hungry dog's tooth to a marrow-bone.   If it once takes hold it 'll never let go. Sell them patents for twenty-five cents a piece, and it's my add-vice to every man to add this vice to his carpenter's tools.

"But scissors and knives! what's the use of talkin' about a little thing like that, that you'll all buy, without askin', when I've got somethin' a mighty sight nicer. I've got the exclusive *and* expensive right in this hull State for a brick-makin' machine. That's the all-firedest thing you ever did see. Now I see there's a great lack of timber about here—it's all perrarie —fust rate for farmin' but troublesome bout buildin' houses. Who wants a frame house, when he can have a nice, genteel brick one? You can make brick so cheap by this here machine I'm tellin' you of, that it's cheaper to have 'em than to go without. This wonderful, surprisin', and valuable, as well as ingenious contrivance takes up the clay, molds it, hardens it, and drops it out ready for use. Two men and one horse can make thousands of thousands in a day, without any other expense than preparin' the clay. Why! I'd like to have said the machine laid up the bricks and built the house itself, but it don't *quite* do that, and I shan't say so. The man that invented that machine deserves to be considered a regular brick himself. Howsumever, I won't detain you no longer to-night. I must pitch in and husk a double portion to make up for lost time. What time is it, Amos? seving o'clock? Speaking of the time, reminds me my teamster will be along in a day or two with a load of first-rate clocks. Good time for anybody to supply themselves that happen to be in need of a cheap, thorough-going time-piece. Warranted to run day and night, but never to run away. Got good ones as low as twelve shillin's, cash,—clocks, you know, never sell on tick. Here, yeou, Amos, set along, and let me set side of Miss Lancaster You see, I'm bashful, and I'm better acquainted with her than I am with the rest, and if I should happen to get a red ear— hello! what's that?—a fiddle! Jemima! how it makes my toes feel. Come, boys, work away; the sooner we're done the longer time we'll have to dance. We 'won't go home till mornin'.'"

Amos had not told any one there was to be dancing; and at the exhilarating sound of old Sambo scraping his fiddle- strings out in the yard, there was a general stir, and great ex-

hilaration of spirits. The corn-husks flew about like feathers.
The prospect of a good supper and a merry dance was sufficient to lower the pile with astonishing rapidity.

Amos had been stealing sidelong glances at Edith's work,
as she deftly peeled down the rustling covering from the
golden beads, in the secret hope that she would chance upon
a *red ear;* but somebody else's eyes were as sharp as his own,
and suddenly Uncle Zeke cried out :

" There ! there ! you needn't try to slip that into the basket
unbeknown. Come, come, Miss Edith, fair play ! You've
got a red ear. Jemima ! but ain't I in luck ? It goes 'round
this way, and I'll get the first one."

" A red ear ?" queried Edith, ignorant of the penalty attached to the finding of that article.

" Yes, ma'am ! and you'll have to submit to be kissed by
the hull crowd, beginning with myself Oh, ho ! but you've
got two red ears now."

" Oh, fie !" cried Edith, beginning to blush, and not knowing just what to do in such an emergency.

" I think Miss Lancaster ought to be excused, seeing she is
in ignorance of the custom, and not ' to the manner born,' "
pleaded Amos, jealously sensitive as to the rude salute of the
company.

" Yeou git out !" exclaimed Uncle Zeke ; " do you think
I'm such a born fool as to lose the only opportunity I'll ever
have, 'less I'm so fortinate as to happen along at the weddin' ?
No, sir ! let Zekiel Pursen alone for gettin' what belongs to
him. Whew ! but ain't I in luck ? Don't be mad, Amos !"
and throwing his arm around Edith's neck, he planted a loud
kiss, fair and square, upon her crimson cheek.

At this instant there was a movement near the door, and
Edith, looking toward it, beheld standing within its huge por-
tals Mrs. Potter, and by her side a middle-aged gentleman—
tall, handsome, haughty-looking, with that perfectly-toned
dress and air of self-possessed repose, which marks the person
accustomed to society. His air, at this instant, however, could
hardly be called one of repose ; a flash of anger, almost of dis-
gust, had passed over his features at the action of the *nonchalant*
Yankee, who was now regarding him with that queer, inquisitive expression peculiar to him.

In one second Edith comprehended that it was her father. An overpowering emotion kept her perfectly silent and still—an emotion which prevented her, at that time, from detecting what Amos felt in his soul, and which gave him a shock and chill like that of being plunged into an ice-hole. If some evil genius had had the liberty of selecting a moment the most *mal à propos* for producing a favorable impression upon the proud and reserved mind of the English gentleman, that evil genius would have selected this especial time.

The rustic employment of the company in which his daughter shared, was not as repelling to him as the rude familiarity of manners implied by the jolly salute of the New Englander.

Not entering into the real spirit of the scene, but standing as a cold, displeased spectator, he judged what he saw in the severest manner.

The letter which James had received that afternoon had been delayed so long by the way that his master was close upon its footsteps. Hardly had Edith left James to his joyful reflections, to return to the husking-bee, before a knock at the front door of his little cottage—a loud, commanding knock to which it was but little accustomed—sent him, with trembling knees and hands, and a "sense" of who it was in his heart, to admit—his master.

An hour spent in giving a *résumé* of the past, and then the two started off in pursuit of the absent child.

A year of emotion was concentrated in the moment of silence following upon Edith's recognition of her father. She felt that a change as entire as it was unexpected had come over the manner of her life. In the whirl of unformed images which confused her brain, one truth arose pre-eminent and stood fixed where all others shifted—her love for Amos. Although her heart yearned toward her father with an instinctive tenderness, she felt as if *her home* was with her lover and the friends of her childhood.

The contempt which had chilled Mr. Lancaster's expression at sight of the rough familiarity of the tall Vermonter, melted away as Edith arose to her feet and looked at him. Always beautiful, always graceful, there was nothing in her to offend his fastidiousness—nothing to cool the glow of love with which he stepped forward and folded her in his arms.

That moment, to James Pipkin, was "the proudest of his life;" standing on the wide threshold, he beheld it with glistening eyes, his little height seeming to reach up an unwonted inch, and the ribbons of his cue fluttering with tremulous joy.

Mr. Potter had hardly shaken hands with Mr. Lancaster, before the restless servant suggested their return home, for fear the quails would be overdone and the master's supper spoiled. In vain Mr. Potter and his wife urged the gentleman to remain and partake of their hospitalities. No, no, he was too weary, too travel-stained ; and Edith, filled with youthful regret for the lost frolic, was obliged to get her bonnet and shawl, and return with them, leaving Amos too angry and disappointed to eat a mouthful of his mother's feast, and to wish the fiddler were in Halifax all the time he was dancing his prettiest with the homeliest girl at the husking.

"Wall, Amos, how 're you enjoying yourself?" asked Uncle Zeke, with a sly twinkle of the eyes, shortly after supper, as the young man led a pug-nosed maiden to her seat after a rather melancholy dance.

"You are enjoying yourself enough for both, I hope," responded Amos ; for Uncle Zeke had proved his talent for "pigeon-toeing" and "cutting wings" equal to that of selling patent-rights ; his heels were as nimble as his tongue ; and he had led off the first dance with a rosy-cheeked girl, with a grand flourish which had given all the idle ones plenty to do in watching him.

"Oh, it's all right with me—only seems to me there ain't so many taller-candles burnin' as there was a while ago. Say, now, don't the barn look ruther gloomy ? A sartain pair of eyes would light it up amazingly. I see by the way you danced the fiddler hadn't any grease in his elbow,—didn't play in time—played too fast for *yeou*—though *I* managed to keep up with him purty smart. Nice man that father-in-law of yourn ; hope to have the pleasure of an introduction some day—he couldn't stop to-night, you know ! He looked so delighted when he saw me a saluting of his daughter—as if Uncle Zeke hadn't the privilege of kissing his own niece, that is to be ! Look out, my boy, or you'll find a high tariff laid on that kind of sweets yerself. I can see as fur by daylight as any other man. *I* go for annexation, and if anybody is opposed to it, he's got to fight it out with me. Je-whillikins! if that fiddler ain't at it again! Suthin's the matter with my butes,—they won't keep still. Git out the way thar, fellers, or my butes 'ill step on you. They're *ruther* small, but they need plenty of room Hail Columbia! where's my girl!" and seizing a smiling lass by the hand, Uncle Zeke was off in another cotillion.

CHAPTER VII

FATHER AND DAUGHTER.

"The course of true love never did run smooth"—never! if it did there would be no stories to write and read, and all young people would be stupidly happy, without ever knowing the delight of being miserable. And so it happened that a great rock dropped suddenly into the silver stream of our young couple's love, damming it up and making it flow out of its quiet channels; but as is the very natural result of such obstructions, it only made it the more wayward, tumultuous, and deep, fretting against the rock as if it hoped to wear it away, foaming and chafing and murmuring loudly, making a very pretty scene for the artist to sketch, but causing the stream itself much discomfort.

Mr. Lancaster took possession of his daughter as entirely, and with as little ceremony as if he were entitled to her by right of having brought her up and cared for her all his life and of course James had no objections to such procedure, but looked with deep delight upon every step taken to restore the young lady to her "proper position." She must return with her father to England, and he was in great haste. He had torn himself from his family and occupations upon hearing of her existence, leaving home so unexpectedly that he felt the necessity of as little delay as possible.

"Sell your farm, James, and go home with us. Sell it for cash, what you can get, and if you are obliged to sacrifice it, I will make good your loss. You will never return here."

"I'd give it, wegetables and all, for a ten-pun' note, afore

I'd be kept in Hamerica, and the young lady gone to her own."

So with James as anxious as her father, what could Edith do ? The clinging of her heart to the family which had been to her as her own, seemed not to be taken into account by those who took the disposal of her doings into their own hands.

"Oh, Mrs. Potter, I do not wish to go at all," exclaimed the young girl, as she related to that person the substance of her interview with her father, the day after the corn-husking. "I shall not be at home in that atmosphere of criticism and cold elegance. I know my step-mother will hate me—I feel it already."

"Better stick to your mother-in-law," suggested Uncle 'Zekiel.

Edith looked quickly into Mrs. Potter's eyes, blushing violently, for her engagement to Amos was of so recent date that she had not accustomed herself to think of the adjuncts. The earnest glance she met brought the tears as well as blushes.

"I love my father as much, almost, as I admire him,—but I can not endure the thought of going home with him," she continued.

"Why not stay with us ?"

Mrs. Potter asked the question quietly. Amos, who had said but little, and who was standing by the window looking moodily out, started, and turned brightly toward his mother and their visitor.

"Yes, Edith, stay with us," he pleaded, while his eyes, his expression, pleaded more for him than his lips. "*His* right is not as good as ours."

"Do *you* think so, Mrs. Potter ?" questioned the young girl. "I know you would not advise me wrongly. He is my father; he has come a great distance to find me. Oh, I felt so tenderly toward him, when we wept together this morning over my mother's grave. Do you think it would be right for me to refuse his love and resist his authority so entirely as to refuse to go with him ?"

"I can't say it would be right, child," she answered, hesitatingly,—"though I might wish it ever so much. It certingly would be ungrateful and hard of you—though we all feel so bad about it. I think you ought to go home with him now, and leave the futur' to decide the futur' If he should be obstinate, and seek his own will rather than your happiness, it would be time enough a year from now, for you to make up your mind. You and Amos is both young enough to afford to wait."

Here Amos made an impatient gesture.

"It's true," persisted his mother. " *You* are old enough, and able enough to take care of a wife, but I wouldn't like to see Edith married 'fore she was eighteen. Thare's one thing sartin—if she likes you well enough to marry you after she's been away from you a year, why you'll be sure of each other's minds, and all the more happy for waitin'. I shall be right sorry to let you go, Edith, but I can't say but I think it's best."

"I think we know our own minds, mother,—at least I know mine—though Edith will see men so much more polished, more learned, wealthier, and so much more worthy of her— it wouldn't be strange if she altered her mind !"

"Don't you feel yourself just as worthy of me as a prince of the realm ?" asked the young girl, archly ; "you know you do, Amos ! You are as proud as the proudest—"

"And if anybody else insinuated he wasn't worthy, we'd pound him till he hollered for mercy," said Mr. Purson. "Ho, Amos ! that ain't the girl to be caught by flourishes and gimcracks. You see I know you better'n he does, Miss Edith."

"Well, one thing is certain," continued the young man, a resolute look settling over his features ; " every thing must be fairly understood. I'm going over with you, Edith, when you are ready, to tell your father of the engagement between us, and ask his consent to its consummation at the end of a year. I know he will be displeased ; but if he objects, then I shall oppose your going at all."

Edith knew, too, that her father would be displeased. Her heart quailed and her hands trembled as she tied her bonnet, but the firm expression of her lover's eyes, so bright with resolve and manly feeling, encouraged her to hope, and increased her admiration as well as love."

"Guess I'll go 'long and talk to Mr. Pipkln about his farm, while you're making the old gentleman uncomfortable. If

he's ready to sell out for a half or a quarter what it's worth,
I'm ready to take it.   I hain't no objection to owning a nice
place next to my friend Potter's, whether I settle down on it
at present or not.   I can sell out any day, or hire somebody
to carry it on.   I had a pursentiment I should make something out of that little weazely old chap the minit I set eyes
on him;" and chuckling at the idea, Mr. Purson started on in
advance of the lovers, not to be, as he remarked, " any hin-
drance to their courtin', seein' their time was short."

The Vermonter's visit to James was much more satisfactory
in its results than that of Amos Potter to Mr. Lancaster.   He
made "a bargain" with which he was delighted, while the
young man succeeded in making no arrangement at all.   The
gentleman was not surprised when asked for the hand of his
daughter by the fine-looking, fine-acting young American,
whose brave bearing he could not but admire, for James had
already informed him of the state of affairs.   He listened po-
litely and not unkindly, for Mr. Lancaster was a gentleman,
and respected the feelings of others too much to injure them
unnecessarily.   But he had not made up his mind, and said
so.   He regretted, more than he cared to express, that his
daughter esteemed her affections already engaged, for he had
mentally chosen for her out of his own circle of acquaint-
ances, and really loved her too fondly to be willing to resign
her to any one who would separate her from him by an ocean,
as well as by differing spheres and pursuits.   But of all this
he would not now talk.   He trusted secretly to time and new
interests to wean her gradually, and make herself the one to
break the bonds between the young pair.   So he listened gen-
tly, said nothing to wound or anger the suitor, but made no
concessions further than to give his consent to a visit one year
from then.   While he invited the young man to visit him
and his daughter at their home, at the expiration of a year,
he requested that there might be no correspondence between
the two in the mean time, on the plea of the youth of Edith,
and refused to consider them as engaged in marriage.

" But we *are* engaged, nevertheless," muttered Amos, under
his breath.   He murmured aloud against the restrictions of a
non-correspondence.   "As for me, Mr. Lancaster, I consider
myself of an age when I can write without indiscret'on to the

.ady of my choice. But if you object to your daughter receiving my letters, of course I shall yield to your will until
she is of age, which she will be in a few months—next July,
I believe."

"Very well,—after that it will be time to decide further."

Edith was present during this interview, and her presence
gave more suavity to her father's manners than they might
otherwise have possessed, for he wished to gain her love, and
had sense enough to feel that harshness toward old friends of
hers would hardly be the means of winning it. She could
find no fault with him ; yet she felt sad and chilled ; her eyes
sought her lover's with a sorrowful sympathy.

Mr. Lancaster saw the looks passing between them. He
pitied them, even while he did not approve. His own youth,
his own fond and wayward love, its brief ecstasy, its long
sorrow, rose vividly before him ; for his glance, as he looked
out of the window by which he sat, fell on the grave of that
other Edith whom he had left there years ago, and of whom
this one was now the counterpart. At that moment it was
not in his heart to reprove the willfulness of young love—
there was something in the silent testimony of that mound of
earth which made worldliness of small worth ; and if he could
have dwelt in its presence always, he might have opened his
heart to the young man, learning to love him for his real worth.

"Your loss is my gain," was the consoling remark of Uncle
Ezekiel, as Amos joined him at the orchard-stile, on their way
home.   "I've driv' an everlastin' tight bargain with old
weazel. He's purty sharp for an Englishman, but I knew he
was bound to sell anyhow, and I just told him my only object in buying at all was to make a bargain,—which it was.
Jerusha ! but it hurt him to let his farm go for ten dollars an
acre, improvements and all,—but he knew his master would
make it up to him. He'll go back quite rich for one of his
class, and will splurge among the servants I expect. I've
done a right smart business since I stopped to your house
one way and another, and if my clocks git along all right, I
shall be in clover. Say, what are you thinking about young
man ? Ker-chunck ! good for ye ! walkin' into a mud-puddle
in broad daylight. Pity your father-in-law couldn't see you
now. I reckon Sister Potter 'll be mad when she sees them

trowsers for her to clean. Look-a-here, young man, jist take your uncle's advice, which is a cheap commodity and always in demand. Always see where your bound fur. Cause you're in one trouble don't walk into another. Cause you're disappinted in love, don't muddy your trowsers."

One week from that day Amos had joined his brother at the lead mines of Galena, and entered into speculation with all his little capital; for his was a nature that could not brook idleness and vain regret. Edith was away—Edith was on the ocean, was in her new and distant home,—and he must work, work, to urge the lagging weeks and months along.

One sweet memory was always with him—the face of Edith at parting, wet with tears, the fond eyes turning to linger upon his with that long look of love and prophetic sadness.

"You'll never marry *her*, I can tell you that, brother," said the practical Daniel, " so you might as well look around among the Galena girls, and forget the proud Englishman's daughter. The fact is, *I* used to fancy Miss Edith amazingly, but I saw plainly that she preferred you, and so I left and contented myself with making a fortune. We'll be as rich as her family if we keep cool, look ahead, and make the best of these mines. Come, come, quit sighing and take to money-making. Wouldn't you like to be worth half a million, Amos ?"

"It would be very agreeable to have that little fortune to offer Edith."

"Edith, pshaw ! you'll marry a hoosier, see if you don't, Amos."

"Lead mines, lead mines ! tell you what it is, boys, I calkilate if there's any shares to spare I'll have a hand in," said Ezekiel Purson, coming out to see how "the boys" were "getting along." "Don't know of anybody t'would like to swop a few shares for some of my patent-rights, do you ?"

CHAPTER VIII.

THE FAITHFULNESS OF TRUE LOVE.

EDITH LANCASTER was becoming initiated into the ways of fashionable people, in her London home. Mr. Lancaster had a beautiful sister married to an earl, a widower with three children by his first wife; the two daughters nearly enough of Edith's age to be society for her, and the son, a handsome and promising youth of twenty-two, who might have set any young girl's heart in a flutter.

Arthur Beverly was the eldest and only son, and would inherit his father's title; he was a high-bred and noble-spirited youth, brilliant, gay, without being dissipated. It was the secret hope, the one ambition of Mr. Lancaster to make a match between his daughter and this son, cousin by courtesy, though not by blood. His wishes upon the subject were confided to no one, not even to his own proud and ambitious wife, who looked upon Edith as an interloper, and whose plans were all centered upon her own son and Edith's half-brother Arthur, named after Arthur Beverly.

It was a great change of circumstance and surrounding to our western heroine—this Arabian-Nights-like flitting from James's cottage and Mrs. Potter's farm-house to her present sumptuous home. It was well for her that she had a perfection of beauty, a delicacy of taste, and a grace of demeanor which enabled her to pass the cold scrutiny of her step-mother and the calm criticism of her titled relatives.

As for the rest, her mother's dress-maker and milliner fitted her out, to fill her new station with all outer propriety of faultless toilet. She was not ushered into society, went to no balls or grand assemblies; but she was frequently at her uncle's house, and saw the people at her father's dinner-table and at the small evening reunions of her mother. Thus she ended quietly into her new sphere, "still as a star," but too

bright and lovely a star to escape notice. The Earl of Beverly admired his niece very much, told his daughters she
would rival them most successfully, remarking to his son
what a fine girl his cousin was—all of which encouraged Mr.
Lancaster in his purpose, and caused him to ignore the existence of Amos Potter, farmer's son and lead-mine speculator,
far away in the Western prairies.

He was unpleasantly reminded of this young man's existence, some seven or eight months after his return to London,
by receiving a letter from him, requesting the privilege of
corresponding with Miss Edith, who was now of age, and in-
closing a letter addressed to her. For a moment—a moment
only, he was tempted to repress the epistle, and write per-
emptorily to him, refusing any further acquaintance. But he
was a man of too much honor; he recalled the duplicity of
his wife, who had played such a part with him and his child;
and ended his reverie over the circumstances by going to
Edith with her lover's communication, and requesting an interview with her, in the library, after she had read it. He
was not blind to the sudden tremor, the warm blush, with
which she had recognized the handwriting.

"She has been so quiet, has seemed so well-content, I hoped
she had seen the impropriety of the affair long ago," he
thought, as he sat waiting her appearance. "I don't like her
blushing—it's suspicious!"

When she came in, her face was so eloquent of what was
passing in her heart, that he saw how faint were the prospects
of driving Amos Potter from her thoughts at present; he
knew that she was becoming tenderly attached to himself, and
he threw himself upon her affection in desiring her to refuse
a correspondence to the young man and to try and forget him.

"But we love each other!" cried Edith.

"You think you love him, my dear child, because he obtained an undue influence over you, before you had opportunities of comparing him with other men. Now, surely, since
you are aware you may have your choice, you will reflect before you allow this matter to go further. Is there not one
whom you already prefer to him—one greatly his superior in
almost all respects? My dear, if Arthur Beverly should offer
you his hand, would you not accept it?"

A crimson torrent rushed up to the girl's cheek and brow.

"Father, is not Amos Potter the equal of Arthur in every thing, except in birth?"

"Birth is every thing."

"No, it is not. I grant you all the advantages of birth and culture, of high station and great fortune—they are not to be despised, and I respect them with all due respect; but there are souls, dear father, to whom God has given a birthright and peerage of their own—they are equal to all things. With the exception of that brilliancy of manners which is so admirable, yet, by no means, all-important, either to happiness or success, I do not see but that my lover is the equal of my cousin. If you would look at him without prejudice, I believe you would recognize his superiority as a man."

Mr. Lancaster regarded the kindling glance and earnest tones of his daughter with surprise; he had never before seen her display a firmness like this she exhibited in defense of Amos; it revealed a new trait in the character he had deemed so plastic. Most men are angered by opposition, no matter how wisely made. He felt a great irritation at this display of independent opinion.

"There is scarcely a girl in England who would not be proud to become the wife of Arthur. There are a hundred mammas maneuvering for him—but he loves *you*, Edith. It's a fact; I have seen it for some time. It will not be many weeks before he will tell you so. He is waiting his opportunity. It is your father's advice and wish that you accept him when he offers himself."

Edith retired to her room to indulge in that luxury of grief to all young girls—"a good cry."

"What are you weeping for?" asked her step-mother, who chanced to pass through the library just after she left it, and who, detecting the subtle atmosphere of a recent disagreement about her husband's manners, had come immediately to Edith to find out what was the cause. Her voice was soft and musical; it seemed to the artless girl, very kind. She felt so lonely, so repelled from her father, that she turned instinctively to the first sympathy which offered itself. She had never loved her step-mother, as much as she had admired her; but Mrs. Lancaster had lately had reasons of her own for winning

her affection and confidence; and when she set her fascina-
tions to the task of winning a person's love, she seldom failed.
The tender smile, the gentle kiss with which she enforced her
question melted the impulsive heart of Edith; she needed *a
mother* so much—and throwing herself upon a bosom which
received her with apparent sympathy, she sobbed aloud.

When the tempest of emotion had spent itself, so that she
could control her voice, she poured into an attentive ear the
story of her engagement to the young American, and of her
father's opposition.

"Why does he oppose your marriage? it is natural he
should be grieved by the prospect of your leaving him for a
home in another hemisphere; but has he any further objection?"

"I believe he has other views for me," stammered Edith,
whose modesty hesitated at avowing what her father had as-
serted.

"Ah! any one in particular? I think I know, my darling—it is the young earl that is to be, is it not?"

The young girl's silence gave consent.

Mrs. Lancaster's thoughts canvassed a wide ground before
she spoke again. She had been pleased at the idea of Edith's
leaving them for a permanent return to her old home, that
herself and her boy might have no rival nor co-heir; but
now she reflected further. If there really was a prospect of
her making so brilliant a match, it might be desirable to help
bring it about; for the honor would reflect upon herself, and
would even be another step in the advancement of her son.
She would be mother to an earl's daughter, would be conspicuous at a splendid wedding, would be enabled to achieve
some social triumphs of her own—visions of diamonds reset,
of a wedding-breakfast, of ceremonies stately and superb, swept
through her mind with bewitching influence, and she decided
to make her fair step-daughter serve to adorn her own brilliancy, like a new jewel set in her tiara.

"It is a tempting prospect; I should think it would turn
the brain of almost any young lady; for Arthur is noble, not
in birth alone, but in all that makes women admire and love
him. If he should honor you with his choice, I should think
you would find him irresistible; I shall be curious to see the

person who could maintain a rivalry with him. But, my
sweet child, if you really love this American—person—"

"Gentleman, mother—why do you not say—gentleman?"

Mr. Lancaster elevated those straight, black brows of hers
with a slight, sarcastic inquiry, which ended in a smile.

"You are entirely capable of judging, dear Edith; yet, perhaps, when you see this hero again, his proportions may have
dwarfed—his heroic attributes may have taken unaccountable
flight. Many a girl laughs and wonders at her 'first love,'
when her judgment has become more mature. I have no disposition to make you unhappy by placing any barriers between you and the object of your love. Yet I have little
doubt that when you meet your *fiancé* after a year's absence,
he will appear to you so totally different from the lover about
whom your fancy has hung clouds of glory, that you will will-
ingly resign him. I believe absence will be the only medicine
your imagination will need."

"I shall never change my mind about Amos," was the firm
reply.

"*Who?*" with a light laugh.

"Amos—Mr. Potter."

"Mr. Amos Potter. Well! Shakspeare says there's nothing in a name, and his authority is not to be despised. No
doubt I shall be just as willing to have the card of Mrs. Amos
Potter, America, brought to me, as that of Edith, Countess of
Beverly, Putnam Square. But, come, let us leave all our
troubles and look at this beautiful robe which has just been
sent home."

The almost imperceptible contempt which colored the gay
badinage of Mrs. Lancaster, was not unperceived by Edith.
Ridicule is more deadly in its small sting to imagination and
even to passion than any sword of tragedy; and from that
day the young girl never spoke, without hesitation, her lover's
name, in the presence of that delicate sarcasm.

The world-wise lady informed her husband, that same
evening, that she knew, better than himself, how to effect the
desired consummation, and unless he wished to bring about
the catastrophe they dreaded, to make no open opposition to
Edith's lover; to allow matters to rest quietly, and *she* would
see they were made no worse; that to oppose love, was to

fan a flame; that fathers never knew how to deal with daughters; if he loved Edith, he must act so as to convince her of his tenderness and win upon her gratitude—for the rest, leave it with her.

It was with that charming joyousness of manner which distinguishes a satisfied mother-in-law elect that she welcomed Arthur Beverly. The family did not invite much company, as they were on intimate terms with the household of Beverly, which prevented their feeling lonely. Mrs. Lancaster gave two or three brilliant *déjeuners à la fourchettes* and *fête champêtres*, which satisfied her ambition to be ranked as an elegant entertainer; the rest of the season she was satisfied to go where she was invited, and to employ the intervals of time in freshening up for another London season. Edith could sit hour by hour and day by day at her chamber-window, overlooking the soft and finished loveliness of an English landscape, dreaming the dreams of youth. Not that she passed all of her time in this delicious idleness. She rode out frequently with her cousins, the daughters of the earl, upon which occasions Arthur invariably made one of the company. They had exhilarating rides, made romantic excursions to distant points of interest, went pic-nicking, had dances in the evening, music, and unceremonious gayety, and some formal dinner-parties now and then.

Every day, when he thought of it on his pillow in the morning, Arthur Beverly resolved to declare his love to his cousin Edith before he slept again; and every evening he wondered what influence it was which had prevented his doing so. Opportunities were not wanting, but encouragement was. Yet Edith admired him; none laughed more gayly at his sallies of wit, none listened more appreciatively to his flights of youthful eloquence. *Why* did she not love him? He had no hint of the existence of that stalwart rival far away; tho fact of such a person being his rival was most studiously kept from him by Mrs. Lancaster.

Free from egotism as Edith was, she could not fail to perceive, after the hints which had been given her, that Arthur fancied her; but never, in a moment of girlish vanity, did she give him any encouragement of which he could afterward accuse her. She was as free from coquetry as her manner of life might be supposed to make her. If she ever looked brightly into the young gentleman's eyes, or smiled her admiration upon him, it was because she liked and respected him, and because he was so brave and accomplished he forced her good opinion. Ah, Amos Potter, you would have left your lead mines had they been mines of gold, and have flown to snatch your beloved away from the dangerous influence of so much that was admirable, had you have had eyes to see through that dreary distance. Or you would have given up at once, in despair, and proudly withdrawn yourself from a rivalry which promised so badly for you!

If there was any one kind of *fête* at which Mrs. Lancaster preferred to shine as hostess, it was a *fête champêtre*. The first two she had given had been successes, weather and all combining with her for the occasion, and she resolved upon another before the cold rains of autumn should have shaken the last roses from the lawn. The young people entered with more zeal into these out-of door amusements than into any other; their taste was freely put into requisition to adorn the grounds of Oakland for charming revelries; snowy tents gleamed out of the emerald lawn; crimson flags fluttered to the breeze; arches and coronals and picturesque effects were happily disposed, and on the auspicious day, soft strains of music melted upon the golden air—even the sun condescended to shine for Mrs. Lancaster—which thrilled every heart, not too calloused to refuse to thrill at any thing, and set the pulses of all the young people dancing madly. No one seemed so cold or so self-content as to refuse to be gay at Mrs. Lancaster's *fête*. "The music and the balmy air, the rich and joyous" day awoke "all impulses of soul and sense." The Earl of Beverly's daughters, fair and stately girls, flitted about like graceful spirits, robed in the light and floating draperies appropriate to the season. Arthur was the embodiment of wit and brilliancy—a diamond, flashing everywhere. His father and sisters could hardly conceal their pride in him. Edith was the delight of all. If the flower-spirit whose soul made beautiful the roses and lilies of the parterres had inhabited her form, she could have been no more gentle and beautiful. Her zephyry azure scarf, her fluttering dress of Indian brown, her elastic step, and happy face, crowned by its golden coronal of hair, with all the beauty of her features and the goodness of expression, made a picture of loveliness which adorned the *fête* with a new satisfaction to all participators. Wherever the blue scarf streamed, there a crowd of young gentlemen gathered, like enthusiastic adherents gathering around the banner of their faith.

An inspiriting march led ardent battalions to the attack of an unresisting banquet. Shortly after this had been stormed and taken, and its effects distributed among the victors, while some of the young people were dancing in a grand *marquee*, Mr Lancaster, with a party of his friends, stood on the lawn near the carriage-drive, discussing the merits of some new agricultural implements, and talking of the crops with the wisdom of amateur farmers. But the ladies were unwilling to allow them these prosy discussions; Mrs. Lancaster, beautiful in a corn-colored dress, with graceful branches of wheat and poppies in her black hair, looking like the goddess of autumn herself, came toward them with persuasions to come and look at the dancers; while, from another direction, Blanche, daughter of the Earl of Beverly, with Arthur and Edith, came up laughingly with a long garland which they threw about Mr. Lancaster.

"Your flowery chain is sweet, but it is not strong enough!" cried that gentleman, as the wreath parted, releasing him from the fairy bondage. "I am already in bonds," with a motion toward his beautiful wife; "but, young ladies, why do you not seek to enchain him whom you have with you?"

"He is captive enough, without chains," retorted Blanche, with a glance at Edith and her brother. "Wherever we fly, he follows."

"A devoted brother—am I not?" asked Arthur.

"And cousin," continued Blanche; at which the company looked at Edith, to enjoy her blushes, but she was not in the least confused. Arthur was almost angry at her for her innocent calmness.

"Jemima! wall! I'm a lucky fellow! I've often thought I was before; and now I'm sure of it—a fool for luck, you know. How *do* you do, Mr. Lancaster? And, bless my eyes, Miss Edith! you're as purty and good as ever! How *do* you do? I don't wonder you look surprised—I'm surprised myself."

The company stared in amused curiosity at the intruder who had come among them unnoticed from a bend in the carriage-drive. For a moment Mr. Lancaster did not call to memory the tall Vermonter who had once before surprised him so unpleasantly,—the next instant a vivid recollection of the husking-bee rose before him, and with it the angry feeling which had then disturbed him. It was Mr. Ezekiel Purson in all the glory of his individuality, and whom no one could ever mistake. Edith blushed with the sudden glow of a thought of Amos, as she thus met one so intimately associated with her old home. Her father had only bowed frigidly, but she held out her hand with a cordial smile, and Mr. Purson shook it heartily. As she looked up she met the quizzical eyes of her step-mother,—they seemed to be asking, along with the arched brows—

"A friend of yours?" and a mortified look passed over her expressive face. Glancing quickly at the others, she read the amused face of Blanche, the haughty look of Arthur, who did not like the familiar air of the intruder. She was apprehensive that Uncle Ezekiel, in the innocence of his heart, would begin to tell her all about Amos and the folks at home, and perhaps refer to her engagement; and anxious as she felt to hear from her lover, she could not endure the idea of having him mentioned in that company by the rough, good-natured American. "They will think all Americans are like Uncle Ezekiel,—when he is almost as much of an oddity at home as he is here," she thought. But she need have entertained no fears of the wisdom of Mr. Purson. If he had no refinement of manner, he had a tact of his own which prevented his shocking the young girl's sensibility or injuring the cause of Amos, which, he had shrewdness enough to know, would not be favored by any forwardness on his part.

"You see," he continued, when he had done shaking hands with Edith, "I'm travelin' in this country sellin' patent-rights. I've got a corn-husker that everybody who sees it is crazy to get. It strips the husks off a bushel a minit, and dispenses entirely with the necessity of huskin'-bees, which is a great savin', but very unfortunate for the girls, especially where red ears are plenty." Here Uncle Ezekiel looked so slyly at Mr Lancaster, that that gentleman could not forbear smiling.

"You see, ladies and gentlemen, I was totally onaware when I came upon these premises, which I must say are rather handsome for *this* country, I should meet with anybody I'd ever seen before; and you may judge of how uncommon tickled I am to meet this young lady, who lived next neighbor to my bosom friends nigh about the best part of her life. The hull country round about has been in mournin' ever since her father found her out and carried her away, which nobody can blame him fur, though everybody is mad as a hornet's nest to think he ever did find out about her. Maybe, if she'd stayed where she was born and brought up, she might have married some of our likely young chaps, which I reckon is rather unprobable, as matters have turned, judging from pres ent appearances," and the gray eyes twinkled upon Arthu. Beverly. "Howsomever, I'm making free to talk about matters of a delicate nature, for which I beg pardon, and will endeavor to confine myself to my legitimate subject, which is— corn-huskers. Before I begin I'd like to ask after the health aud happiness of my pertickerler friend, Mr. Pipkin."

"Oh, Mr. Pipkin is very well, and very happy—quite at the summit of contentment," answered Edith.

"Glad to hear it, glad to hear it. He was a *very* particker ler friend of mine, Mr. Pipkin was; and when he went away he left me his farm for a trifling consideration, scarcely worth mentioning—which I regard as a very striking proof of friendship. We used to quarrel on politics, because, like all good men, we both swore by our own country. He swore by Queen Victory, as he'd oughter, and I stuck to George Washington. He was a fust-rate fellow, a little cowardly, but he made up for that in bragging after the danger was over. Lord, how I laughed once to see him take to his heels at the sight of a stick in the water, which he mistook for a black snake, and when I hollered after him what it was, he said he was running for a hazel-bush to thrash it. A great fellow James was, for a little one, which reminds me of the crops of corn he used to raise on that bottom-land, which puts me in mind to speak of my corn-huskers. See here, gentlemen; I'll just trouble you to examine the model," and Mr. Purson drew forth the model and began explaining it to those nearest him.

The gentlemen crowded around to look at it, amused at the

volubility of the Yankee, as well as interested in the patent corn-husker, as many of them raised more or less corn upon their estates. "Fact is, gentleman, I set a good deal of store by that concern. Not that I haven't got other things to sell that are invaluable. I've got the right of a steam-plow that just walks over the land itself, and a drill that follows after it of its own accord, and plants the seed already sprouted. I've got a scarecrow that's warranted to throw every bird that sees it into convulsions, followed by catalepsy and death. I've got a reaper that goes through wheat-fields and can't be stopped till the grain is in the barn, all thrashed, weighed, and measured, and ready for market. But I ain't a-going to recommend these things,—they recommend themselves. All I ask is the privilege of showin' 'em. Everybody takes 'em, some as they would take a pretty wife—without persuading. Yankee notions, every one of 'em. I've got an idea for the ladies, too,—Ezekiel Purson would be false to the first emotions of his nature if he forgot the interests of the fair sex. Madam," with a flourishing bow to Mrs. Lancaster, "permit me the privilege of entering your laundry, and for a sum too trifling to be mentioned, I will play the part of an Irish banshee there, doing up the work in the absence of the maid. I will put a machine in there that will sort the dirty linen, wash, rinse, dry, clear-starch, and iron and air, and be ready to send up again, for the whole establishment, in less than three hours from the time it came down. Fact!—no mistake! It can be done. Which puts me in mind of my corn-husker. You see the principle upon which it works, gentlemen. How many of you are going to order one. They're cheap. I get 'em manufactured fast as they're ordered. Gives employment to your own mechanics, you see. Duty to take 'em. How many of you—give me your orders, gentlemen."

"Call upon me to-morrow, Mr. Purson, I shall have leisure to talk with you then, I'm engaged at present, as you see."

"Engaged, hey?—pretty good for a married man. How is it with you, Miss Edith, you engaged too? I calkilate you are by the looks of some of these youngsters round about. Wall, I hope you'll do as well as you desarve. Any more gentlemen like to have me give em a call?"

The Earl of Beverly indicated such a wish.

" Thank'ee—'twon't be lost time to either of us. And now, with your permission, Mr. Lancaster, I'll make a call on my old friend, Mr. Pipkin, if he isn't too busy to see me."

" I presume he'll be pleased to see you. He is probably taking lunch in the marquee yonder, and will doubtless invite you to join him."

With a circular bow that included the whole company, Mr. Purson passed on in the direction pointed out to him. Edith looked after him wistfully; she longed to follow him and inquire all about good Mrs. Potter, and Mr. Potter, who had tossed her in his arms when she was a child, about the house, the farm, the pigs, and chickens even—while the very thought of Amos, and of hearing directly from him, made her heart beat in her throat. She was determined, at all hazards of the displeasure of her father, to seek an interview with Mr. Purson before he left the grounds. The very sight of his ungainly form had recalled her old home so vividly, as to make her homesick. She scarcely heard the amused remarks of her friends upon this *bona fide* specimen of a Yankee.

Arthur Beverly seconded her attempts to steal away from the company ; but his purpose was different from hers.

" Let us go to the rose-thicket and see if there are any more of those lovely tea-roses in bloom. A cluster of them would look well in your girdle, Edith, and be very appropriate."

As the young couple wandered away together, the two fathers looked after them and then at each other.

" They make a pretty pair," said the Earl.

" Do you think so ?—so do I," responded Mr. Lancaster, excessively gratified ; and the matter was understood between them thereafter. The *fête champêtre* took on a rosy glow to the proud parents.

In the mean time the two most interested, flitted through the fragrant recesses of the rose-thicket in strange silence. Arthur was thinking of Edith, and she was wondering how she could manage to shake off her companion before arriving at the marquee, where the servants were feasting upon the remnants of the banquet, and near which they now were. She wanted an uninterrupted talk with Mr. Purson, unrestrained by any third presence.

" You are growing pale," spoke Arthur at length ; " you are ot bright as you were an hour ago. What is the matter ?"

She looked at him, surprised by the unusual tone in which he spoke; his voice was impatient, trembling, capricious ; his eyes drew the true answer from her lips before she was aware.

"I am homesick, Arthur," and the tears began to roll down her cheeks. "Do you think it strange ? Remember, this is to me a new land and new people. I love them—but I love my old associates, too. Do you think it strange I should sometimes pine for them ?"

"No—no! but I wish you would grieve for them no longer, Edith,—or, if you can not entirely forget them, I wish you would allow me to be your comforter. When we are married, Edith, you shall go to America for a bridal-tour. Will not that be pleasant ?" and he tried to take her hand, and to laugh lightly, as if he hoped to storm her heart and carry it by force of assurance.

"I shall grow weary waiting, if I have to wait till then."

He wondered if this were not the coquetry of a young maiden, and looked to see the conscious roses blush in her cheeks; but she was grave and firm, though her eyes were downcast.

"Can you be in earnest, Edith ? I know I am not worthy of you; no living man is worthy of you—but I hoped you would love me, as I love you—wildly, sweetly, for life, death, and eternity—"

"Hush ! Arthur, you must know all now, since you have said so much. I am already plighted — my lover is in America."

"I never suspected it—no one ever hinted it."

"Because they hoped I would forget him and learn to love another—to love you, Arthur, if you should honor me with your choice. You are good and noble, I acknowledge it—but I love my plain, untitled friend—the boy who grew up with me from childhood. I may never marry him, if my father wills it so ; but I will be true to him—I will never marry another."

"Well, Edith, I can not reproach you, for you have never encouraged me. But I wish I had known this before—before I had allowed my heart to fix itself upon you. It will be a death-struggle with me, almost, to tear it away now."

She admired him at that moment more than ever before.

The sincerity of his disappointment was proven more by the dignity of his grief than it would have been by any passionate protestations.

"Any woman who had a heart to give away could not refuse it to you, cousin Arthur," she said timidly, as if she hoped this pretty flattery would be some consolation to him.

"You wish to speak to that roving Yankee," said Arthur, attempting to smile; "I see it in your face. Shall I go and find him?" and without waiting for her answer, he went toward the marquee.

"So generous!" murmured Edith, looking after him.

Presently the long strides of Mr. Purson scattered the leaves from the amazed roses as he brushed by them.

"I'm in luck, Miss Edith. There was a very handsome young gentleman told me you wished to speak with me, at which I was so beside myself with delight that I let fall a piece of the breast of the chicken, dropped knife and fork, and run. I rather guess Amos would be in a peck of troubles if he seen what I saw to day—don't think he'd sleep well of nights. Mighty nice young feller—goin' to be an earl some day—handsome and very genteel. James is greatly tickled at it."

"At what, Mr. Purson?" and Edith half-frowned, half-smiled.

"Why, at the prospect of his young lady wearing a coronet upon her pretty head, some day. Bless me! what'll Mrs. Potter say, to think she's had the honor of dandling a future countess in her arms, and made pinafores and frocks for her? She'll have it to tell to her grandchildren, when she gets some to tell it to. Just think of her tellin' Daniel's little girls about the little countess that used to chase the chickens round the yard, like an out-and-out republican."

"How is Mrs. Potter? I wanted to ask after her."

"Mrs. Potter?—oh, she's as well as ever—quite hearty—or was the last time I seen her, which was the week before I sailed, which was about a month ago. Come over in a mail-steamer—only nine days a stepping across; been a kind of comin' around toward this place ever since I got here."

"And Mr. Potter—how is he?"

"Mr. Potter?—oh, *he's* right smart. Talks about you considerable—misses you dreadfully. He's got a warm heart, friend Peter has, though; he's mighty quiet, and uses few words. *That's* about the only p'int in which he and I resemble each other—he ain't much of a talker, and neither be I. Mostly when we settle down of an evening to have a little social chat around the fire, or by the door in summer-time, he's tellin' over some of the little pranks and cunnin' doin's of the little girl that used to be around there like a lost fairy. Potter ought to have had some girls of his own—he fancies 'em so much. I hope when his boys marry they'll choose wives that'll be good to the old man."

Edith's lip was trembling by this time.

"How's old Brownie, Mr. Purson?"

"Smart. But he don't appear to have so many antics as he used to—misses the mistress that used to ride him so gayly. He's settling down into a staid old horse, who goes to market and behaves himself generally."

"Has Daniel been home to stay any, since I came away?"

"No, only a spell about Christmas and New Year's. He's getting rich as fast as a man can, Daniel is—doing first-rate. He'll be wuth enough to buy out this estate before five years."

How provoking he was! didn't he know that she wanted him to speak of Amos, and didn't he purposely forbear even to mention his name? He was a rude creature who had no consideration for the delicacy, the shrinking sensitiveness of a maiden—and so, with the blood dyeing her forehead, and her voice faltering, Edith inquired:

"And Amos—how is he?"

"Amos! oh, pretty well, thank you, Miss Edith. I s'posed you'd forgotten him entirely. Shall I tell him you asked after everybody, even the old horse, before you remembered him?"

"Just as you please, Mr. Purson. If you want to make mischief between lovers, you'll only be like the rest of the world," and she pouted prettily. "You know, as well as I do, that I've been waiting for you to tell me all I was perishing to know."

"Did, hey? and how did I know, I'd like to know? I've seen things, since I come to these parts, would make a man careful of obtruding information before it was asked for. That step-mother of yours is a mighty sharp woman, and your

fathcr has a killing polite way of snubbing folks. I don't
blame him, to be sure ; and he's a fine gentleman, and very
fond of his only daughter, and would like to see her make a
grcat match. I reckon he's further than ever from wishing to
see her married to our Amos. And besides that, and wuss
than all, Miss Edith, young ladies themselves are sometimes
onaware of their own minds when they accept the first feller
that asks them,"—and Mr. Purson threw a sudden searching
glance at his companion ;—" and afterward, when a finer one
comes along, conclude they were mistaken, and give the first
one thè slip."

" Well ! who has seen a finer one than Amos ?" asked the
young girl coolly, patting her feet upon the green sward.

" That earl's son is a splendid man, I'll own up ; he's got
fincr manners than Amos, he's full as good-lookin', and he's
goin' to have a title. He's a *real* gentleman, too—none of
your purtendcd kind, and I liked him as soon as I sot eyes
on him. But I felt sorry for Amos."

" You need feel sorry for Amos no longer, Mr. Purson. I
haven't changed my mind a shade about him. But, as I re-
alize more and more, I may ncver be able to fulfill my engagement with him. If I am not, I shall die an old maid,
that's all !"

" Sho !" exclaimed Uncle Zeke, " that ain't in the natur'
of girls ;" and he finished off his thoughts with a low whistle.
" But it does me good to hear you say so, though I don't believe a word of it. Not but what you believe yourself *now*,
ut two or thrce years from now you'll be laughing at the
Idea. Howsumever, I'll tell Amos you said it."

" I'll tell him myself before long. Is he not coming to see
me at the appointed time ? I am beginning to count the
days."

" Wall, thc fact is," and the speaker lowered his voice, " I
expect he'll come, for Amos is plucky, and will stand by his
rights. If he's dismissed, he means to be dismissed by you.
But he's low-spirited. The day or two before I started, he received a letter from your step-mother, telling him, very polite-
ly, that he needn't trouble himself to take such a long journey,
with the hopes of continuing his acquaintance with you, for
you were to be married within a year, to the only son of the

Earl of Beverly—'a match,' she added, with a cruel meaning, 'in every respect worthy of our good and beautiful child.'"

"Is it possible!" murmured Edith, in astonishment.

"So you see Amos was a good deal took down, for he hadn't been any too hopeful before ; but he said he should come at the appointed time—angels nor devils couldn't keep him away, and he'd hear it from your own mouth before he'd believe it. I suddenly took a notion I'd like to travel in another country, and sell patent-rights enough to pay my way ; and maybe I could make it convenient to find out which way the wind was blowin',—and that's jest about all that brought me to England, Miss Edith, I tell the truth. I was makin' money faster to home than I could make it anywhere else. I've got some shares in them lead-mines, too ; but that's a kind of business that'll take care of itself for a while, and, I reckon, a little forrin travel will be immensely advantageous. I need polishin' wuss'n a rusty stove, and I expect a forrin brush will lay it on faster'n any thing else—hey, Miss Edith ? Time I get rubbed up to the required brilliancy, I expect to start off with a new patent to sell—patents of nobility. They'll bring a tremendous price—I shall make my everlastin' fortin."

Edith smiled at her unique companion, but her heart was still full of questions, and time was precious.

"How has Amos passed the time since we parted ?—Has he been at home ?—Is he well ?—Does he—think of me ?"

"He's lookin' better than ever—growing more manly-like. He hasn't been to home much—been with Daniel up to the mines. He's makin' money like dirt. 'Tain't probable anybody else knows what he's thinking about. 'Still waters run deep.' He's got to be a perfect steam-engine to work, and I believe he does it to pass away the time. My heart's sot on that boy, Miss Edith. I think more of him than Daniel, or anybody else. I've no chick or child of my own, being an old bachelor who's the victim of unrequited love, and I've jest taken Amos into my heart. He'll be my heir, if I make a fortin'—and of course I shall, with all my patent-rights. Catch 'Zekiel Purson lettin' anybody get ahead of him ! And so I'm glad you think your going to stick to him, whether you succeed at it or not. I'll let him know what you've said."

"I shall see him in October," said Edith.

"My dear child, our guests are leaving. They wish to make their farewells to us. You have been absent longer than is quite proper," and Mrs. Lancaster hurried toward Edith, of whom she had evidently been in search. She did not condescend to see Mr. Purson at all, addressing her as if no other person were present.

"I beg your parding, madam, it's me that's to blame for keeping her. You see, I've been explaining the patent washing-machine to her—and though she is a lady born, I must say she listened as perlitely as a laundry-maid;" and he looked impudently into the black eyes which flashed their fiery scorn upon him.

"Come, my darling, your cousins are already gone."

"Hope you'll allow me the pleasure of settin' up a machine in the laundry of your ladyship's villa, and order another for your house in town. You'll never regret it—fact, madam, though you live a thousand years, and have washing done by it all that time. It supersedes elbow-grease entirely; it'll even wash the stains out of a soiled conscience, if it's well-soaped first—fact! or 'Zekiel Purson wouldn't say it;" but 'Zekiel Purson was talking to the air, for mother and daughter had disappeared.

CHAPTER IX.

A LONG-LOOKED-FOR ARRIVAL.

THE October in which Edith expected her lover came and went, and brought her no tidings. The family were returned to town, and Edith was to be formally introduced into society that winter; an epoch in her life which she would have experienced with the usual brilliant anticipations of her age and circumstances, had not her whole soul been so wrapt in expectation and suspense. Her father and mother were extremely kind and indulgent, seeming as if quietly bent upon rewarding her for some supposed sacrifice, or making amends for some secret wrong. With such a superb home, such tender parents, and such joyous prospects, it would have been almost impossible for Edith to have been unhappy. Yet it was equally impossible for her to be contented. Every call at the door, every ring of the bell, or announcement of company, made her heart beat violently and her color change. She was waiting—constantly waiting—and for one who waits, the affairs which surround them have but a partial interest.

She had not seen Arthur Beverly since the day of the *fête champêtre.* He had started off the following day for a tour in Scotland, and the abruptness of his departure, along with the irritability with which he repelled questioning on the subject, led to the inference that he had been refused. His proud sisters, who adored him, thought such a thing an impossibility, and would give no credence to it, though they mischievously tormented him with it. Mr. and Mrs. Lancaster were deeply chagrined, as they more than suspected the truth. Week after week passed by and he did not return; his father received frequent letters from him, full of accounts of reckless adventures, of boating on the sea, fishing in the lakes, climbing the mountains, of sleeping in peasants' huts, and living for days on oatmeal and curds. Poor Arthur Beverly! he was un-

happy—he was really unhappy and in despair. And when
he felt how miserable he was, how little he had to look forward to, since the only woman he ever could love was pledged
to another—how little sunshine there was in the sky—how
mocking the desires and aspirations of his youthful manhood
—he was certain that his face must betray the wretchedness
of his soul, and he expected to grow pale, thin, perhaps to
find gray hairs coming and premature wrinkles. He hoped
if ever he should again meet Edith, that the silent misery of
his aspect would reproach her with the ruin she had wrought.
He plunged into chasms, climbed rugged rocks, walked wearisome miles, eat coarse fare,—all of which, unfortunately for
the sublimity of his cause, had an opposite effect to that which
he expected to follow. The pure air of the Scottish mountains, the cool waters of the lakes, the vigorous exercise, the
novel life, the plain food, acted like a medicine upon his dis-
eased mind as well as upon his physical powers. Despite of
youthful resolve to be unutterably wretched, despite of the
most bitter despair, his cheeks grew red, his muscles grew
strong, and he found himself gaining so deplorably in flesh,
that the prospects were he should have to reproach the young
lady with the mute appeal of thirty pounds of added weight,
instead of that appalling thinness which he had confidently
expected.

However, of this, Edith as yet knew nothing. His friends
were urging his return in time to be present at the ball at
which she was to make her formal entrance into society.

It was the brief, dim December afternoon preceding this
ball, which was given by Mrs. Lancaster. The house had
been beautifully decorated, Mr. Lancaster giving *carte blanche*
for an occasion in which he had so much fatherly pride.
The odor of costly flowers filled the alcoves and staircases;
and already was nothing wanted to complete the effect of
splendor and elegant taste, but the magic of the gas-lights.

Edith was in her room, preparing to dress. Her mother
was not content to leave her to the hands of her maid upon
so important an occasion, but came in frequently to see that
all things were making proper progress.

An exquisite dress of white crape, over plain white silk,
with some simple trimmings of *fuschias*, was displayed upon

the bed. Instead of feeling exhilarated, Edith began to be de-
pressed. The silver-steel grate threw out a pleasant glow
over the room, but out of the parted curtains she had a
glimpse of the dim, clouded day, gray and gloomy. It was
not time to dress for hours. She took a book and went to
the window to read, but she did not become interested in its
contents, and chose rather to look at the low-hanging sky
and the tall spire of a cathedral not far away, whose top was
lost in the chilly mist. Casting her eyes to the street below,
she watched the tide of carriages setting home to dinner with
their wealthy occupants. It was too aristocratic a neighbor-
hood to be crowded, and but few people passed on the side-
walk, as the day was not fair enough to attempt walking for
pleasure. Presently her glance rested on a person going
slowly by on the opposite side of the street; there was something in the air, the step, the figure, which thrilled her before
she had time for thought.

"Fie! how could I allow myself to be so mistaken," she
murmured, sinking back to her place again. "And yet how
closely it resembled him. Ah! he has turned—he is coming
back—looking up at this window—it is—it *is* Amos!"

She would have thrown open the window and called to
him, she was so excited, had not her step-mother came in
just then, and leaning over her shoulder, looked out, saying:

"There will be no rain to-night. It is a fine night for the
ball, my dear. Every thing is propitious. Come away from
the window, love, don't you see that person staring at you
from across the way?"

"Well, he can not harm me, can he, with this crystal barrier
between us?" laughed Edith, with rather a tremulous voice, striv-
ing to conceal her agitation, and bound to give some signal to
Amos to convince him that this was the house he was looking
for, and that it was she, his own Edith, who was smiling
down at him from the window. She expected every moment
that he would come across, knock at the door, and send up
his card,—that plain "Amos Potter" which her mother
sneered at. But he passed on, when he saw another face,
and made no sign. Edith wondered at this. Her mother insisted upon her leaving the window and not allowing herself
to be stared at. She did so, but her ear was strained to every

sound; she expected to be summoned to the drawing-room every moment, and sat with bright eyes and high-beating heart, unable to do any thing but wait. There was no formal dinner in the dining-room that day; at twilight a servant brought her a dainty lunch; but she could not eat,—she felt as if she could live for ever without food, so etherealized was she by happiness. For she felt that Amos would be at the ball that night. Surely, since he had come, he would not delay calling later than till evening. How provoking it would be if he should come early, as he probably would, not knowing of the festivity, and should be kept waiting while she was dressing. Or worse still, if the footman, knowing the ladies were engaged, should tell him so and not admit him. She flew down to tell Thomas to admit a gentleman who should inquire for her father or her, as she expected a friend.

"If mademoiselle dresses so early, her toilet will not be so perfectly fresh," expostulated the maid, whom she was hurrying beyond her ideas of propriety.

"Ah, but I will be so careful, Margaret; I will not disturb a single fold. And you may keep the flowers till the last moment. Only arrange my hair and dress, so that if a friend whom I expect calls before the hour for company, I can see him."

"Mademoiselle will surpass herself to-night. Her cheeks are like roses, and her eyes like diamonds."

"Are they, Margaret? I am so glad of it. I wish to look my best to-night."

"Of course,—it is your first ball, mademoiselle. And I have heard that your cousin, the young heir of Beverly, has returned from Scotland, and will be here to-night;" and the maid gave a sly look at her young mistress.

"Will he? I was not certain of it," replied Edith, with a light laugh. She could afford to laugh at this arrow which fell so wide of the mark.

She could afford to be happy too, now—to welcome her first ball with an unequalled delight.

"My child, you are lovely—perfectly dazzling. I am afraid I shall be vain of you to-night," said Mrs. Lancaster, coming in; "see what I have for you,—this bouquet. Could any thing be more appropriate—more tastefully arranged? I suspect it is from Arthur, though there was no name came with the gift."

Edith took it with a trembling hand ; some subtle magnetism told her it was from another.

"You need not look for a note," laughed Mrs. Lancaster ; "I searched its sweetness for some written hint of the donor —but the flowers tell their own story. I presume you will see the giver to-night. ("I presume I shall," thought Edith). Arthur has returned on purpose to do this occasion honor."

"I wonder if I really am looking so well—or does my mother flatter me," thought the young *debutante*, regarding herself in the great mirror. The reflection she saw there gave her a feeling of girlish exultation in her own beauty—in the thought that Amos would meet her under such happy circumstances—would think she had improved, and love her better than ever.

"You are dressing very early—you will be greatly fatigued. You had better rest yourself in this arm-chair, toast your feet before the fire, and forget for a while all about the ball."

Restless as she was, Edith tried to obey ; and did indeed succeed in forgetting the ball in a dream of her lover.

"It is strange he delays his call so long ; if it were me, I could not do so—I could not delay one moment. Hark ! no—not him !" and she sank back disappointed for the twentieth time.

Margaret left the room to obtain her supper. Moved by some unaccountable impulse, some mysterious magnetism, Edith stole to the window, drew aside the curtain, and looked down upon the damp pavements, now glimmering in the lamplight. There she beheld the same familiar figure pacing slowly and looking toward her window. She gazed at it earnestly, forgetful that her own form was betrayed by the brilliant light in her room. The person, whoever he was, and whom she felt certain was Amos, stopped and returned her gaze. He could see that lovely form, in its white robe and flower-crowned hair, distinctly ; the roll of an approaching carriage warned Edith of the seeming impropriety of her conduct ; she dropped the curtain and withdrew.

"Why does he not cross the street ? is he waiting to meet me first in a crowd ? I should have thought his heart would

have prompted him to seek me less publicly at first," and
walking uneasily about her apartment, she pressed the flowers
he had sent her, murmuring to herself, as in anticipation:

> " Oh, fluttering heart, control thy tumult,
>   Lest eyes profane should see
>   My cheek betray the rush of rapture
>   His coming brings to me !"

" Your father is waiting in the library to criticise your toilet
before the guests make their appearance," and Mrs. Lancaster
placed fan and handkerchief in her daughter's hand, and they
descended.

" I can only command; I can not criticise," remarked the
father, when his child stood blushing and smiling before him.
" But there is a summons at the door, and we must prepare
to let our friends do the criticising."

"*I* planned the dress, in all its details, and, of course, it
would be perfect. But how am *I* looking, Edwin ?"

" Superb, as usual."

" It was Arthur who came in, I know," continued Mrs.
Lancaster. " He will want Edith to himself the first half-
hour. Let us hasten, my darling, or our guest will find no
welcome."

Yes! it was Arthur; and the heart of Edith sank low,
from the high tide which was swelling it, for she thought it
was Amos. Hardly had the hostess and her daughter taken
up their station at the head of the brilliant suit of rooms, when
Arthur and his sisters entered.

" We have come early, fair cousin, to assist you at these
trying ceremonials," said Blanche, gayly.

" It is very kind of you, and very comforting to me." responded Edith.

" We have brought with us a traveled gentleman, lately
from the wilds of Scotland," said Eleanor, presenting Arthur,
with mock gravity. " If he forgets the decorum proper to
the place, and stalks about like a Highland laddie, you will
excuse him. His business in Scotland was to die of a broken
heart; you see how frightfully near he has come to suc-
ceeding."

It was poor payment for all he had suffered to be conscious
that he was looking the picture of health; but as Arthur met

the merry glance of Edith, neither could forbear smiling. The
heroic is not always tragic. In the fine light of his eye, albeit
it smiled, the young girl read deeper meanings than of old;
there was a look about the brow and lips as of a man capable
of high resolves; whether his sisters perceived it or not, she
saw that his rough tour had conferred real benefit upon
him.

Of course Edith danced first with Arthur. The idea seemed already to have gone abroad that the two were betrothed;
Mrs. Lancaster received several congratulations from envious
mammas, which she disdained with negatives which gave
consent.

In that atmosphere of music, light, sparkling of jewels, and
odor of flowers, the breath of which intoxicates like the eating of hasheesh, Edith was ushered triumphantly through the
grand arch of the first ball into that charmed and fairy world,
(to those outside of it) "society." Not the least taint of her humble bringing-up clung to her garments. She proved herself
her father's child; and he was prouder of her than before, if
possible. The sweet animation which filled her, at the beginning of the evening, gave place to a despondency which she was
obliged to make an effort to conceal, as Amos came not—and
thus she learned the great lesson of "society" so early—that
success depends upon concealing your real self, not express-
ing it.

"Mademoiselle is fatigued; she will feel in better spirits
after a good sleep. She must not stir from bed until twelve
o'clock," said Margaret, as she undressed her young mistress
in the gray dawn.

"Oh, yes, Margaret. I must be up by ten or eleven—do
not fail to call me."

She needed no one to call her, however, for, after a deep
sleep of three or four hours, she started wide awake with the
thought that Amos was not very far away, and could not close
her eyes again.

"Has any one inquired for me this morning?" she asked
her maid, as she summoned her at ten o'clock, after tossing
about the last hour or two, unable to rest.

"I presume not. To be sure I do not know, not having
seen Thomas, but I've heard of no one; and no one of made-

moiselle's friends would be rude enough to call so early, I'm sure."

Edith thought of the hours of sunny brightness and fresh air that she and Amos used to live, under those blue Western skies, before this time of the day; and felt that he would not have been conscious of the terrible blunder it would be to be seen out of doors before one o'clock in misty London, in a locality so exclusive as this.

"I have been mistaken. Now, that I reflect upon it, I *must* have been foolishly mistaken. Of course Amos would not promenade, in that manner, before the house, and never make himself known. It has been some idle fellow, and I have fancied a resemblance in their figures and walk!" And as the day wore on, she tried to persuade herself of her ridiculous mistake, and chided her too-eager fancy for leading her hopes astray.

A tide of calls, billets, bouquets, etc., set in, which claimed her attention irresistibly, however she wearied of them; and toward the close of the day, among other notes brought to her by the obsequious Thomas, was one toward which she felt attracted as magnetically as she had toward the window the previous day. She had just left the dinner-table with her mother and one or two lady-guests, who had begged to open her notes without regard to them; and she instinctively turned her face from them, before daring to break the seal of this. She knew that bold, handsome chirography, though it had been long since she had seen it. Her name, written by that hand, had laughed at her from school-boy slates, from winter-snows, from smooth, white bark of trees, and every inviting surface upon which the ingenuity of a boy could fasten it.

With fingers trembling with impatience, she opened the envelope and read:

"I have traveled nearly four thousand miles, and been rewarded by a glimpse of your shadow, flung against a dancing curtain. Now I will go back over the four thousand miles, which will stretch out into greater length than when hope and love led me. Nevertheless, my native land is fair, and there are truthful maidens in it, no doubt. I have heard of your betrothal to the future earl. I have seen him—he is very attractive, and I do not blame you. Know this, Edith Lancaster, if all the haughtiness of all his family and all your own were matched against my burning American pride, it would not equal it. I will not beg favors. If you are free, so am I, and God bless you. "A. P."

She repressed the cry which rose to her lips, and even forced back the color to her cheeks, and after lingering a few moments indifferently, made her apologies to her mother and guests, and left the drawing-room. Hastening to her own apartment, she sat down to her writing-desk, and wrote:

"How dare you judge me thus, Amos, without hearing from me, or trying to hear from me the truth? I am betrothed to no one, unless it be to you. You wrong me bitterly by supposing it. If my father has wounded your pride, I am sorry for it; but love should be nobler than pride—and stronger. It is with me. It is you who have cast me off—you have not even given me your address, that my denial might reach you. "EDITH."

She sealed her note and bade Margaret go out and drop it in the nearest post. There was no address but London P. O., and she felt that his chances were small for ever receiving it.

"It is cruel—cruel of him to give me no chance to justify myself. His pride, if he only knew it, is just as ugly and arrogant in its way as my father's is in his."

This was a very truthful reflection of our heroine's—a bit of wisdom imparted to her by trouble, which is one of our safest teachers; but as no perfection exists amid mortals, neither was Amos perfect, but weak where he regarded himself as noblest, which also is not an unusual mistake of humanity.

Edith looked in vain, with an anxiety which made her thin and pale, for an answer to her note—it never came.

Then her gentle spirit rebelled. She felt wronged and unhappy—felt that her father, who should have tried to make her happy, had conspired against her—felt that her lover, who should have trusted her against the world, had deserted her.

And all this time Arthur Beverly had renewed his visits—was so gentle, so deferential, so considerate, so devoted, that she began to feel that he was her only friend.

CHAPTER X.

UNCLE EZEKIEL'S LETTER.

DON'T want to buy any soap, do you, madam? I know you do, before you speak. You can't help wanting to buy *this* soap—it's magic soap,—it's got all the essence of sweetness and the secret of beauty combined. 'Tain't made of any vulgar ingredients,—no ile and alkili, no greese and ashes in this soap. It's compounded of proper parts of the otter of fragrance and the spirits of loveliness combined. It's lilies and roses biled down and run in a mold. It'll make a dark complexion snow white, and an ugly woman as beautiful as the goddess of love—what was her name?—but that's nothin' to you, as anybody can see, who are young and pretty, and fair as a rose yourself. But don't you want to always *stay* so?—of course you do. Then buy my soap. It'll keep you as fresh as you are now, a hundred years. Wrinkles are seart out of the house where it is, and freckles hide their diminished heads, ashamed of themselves. It's the very fountain of youth,—a lather made of this soap is what Cortez and all them Spanish fellows were after, instead of that fountain of youth, if they'd only have had the sense to know it, and had held on till I came along with it. I invented this soap to please the fair seet, and perpetuate their charms. There ain't a smell of wintergreen nor cinnamon about it; it's fit for the noses of Portman Square—a very delicate soap, as smooth as cream and as sweet as sugar. *Do* let me persuade you just to look at a cake of it—you can't refuse it if you only see it, as the odor of it reaches your olfactory nostrils,"—and the itinerant, with his basket of soaps and fancy articles, pressed toward the carriage into which Edith had just stepped.

"Clear out, you impudent rascal!" said the coachman from his box, flourishing his whip as if to bring it down on the shoulders of the tall, ragged fellow who had dared to press his wares upon the attention of his young lady.

"Nay, Wilkins, do not be severe upon him," expostulated Edith, looking out; "I will humor him to look at his wonderful soap."

"I knew your ladyship would the minit I looked at your beautiful face. You'll never regret buying a box containing a dozen cakes of this *exquisite*, odoriferous, delightful, and altogether unequaled saponaceous compound."

"As eloquent as ever, Uncle Zekel," said Edith, in a low voice, as she pretended to interest herself in the basket.

"Sho! knew my voice, I expect. Don't think I've sunk so low, Miss Edith, as to sell soap for a livin'. I've just adopted this mode of gettin' around, in the hopes of being able to speak to you. Your servants are so awful stuck-up and careful, they don't let no peddlers into your hall. I've been trying, in one way and another, for a month, now, to get to speak to you. Amos is in hot water—also in Greece or Jerusalem, or some other ancient place where he hadn't ought to be."

"What hot water is he in!" and she examined the soap carefully, while the coachman regretted the kind-heartedness of his young mistress, which so frequently made her listen to beggars, and buy their wares of itinerants.

"Oh, nuthin' in pertickeler, only I knew what a fool he made of himself going off without seein' *you*. You see, your father wouldn't admit him, nor allow him to call upon you. What do you think of that soap now, madam?—delicious, ain't it, the quintessence of soap, no mistake! I told him he ought to be ashamed of himself to be so easily tuck down —he'd no business to flat out without insistin' on seeing *you*, and getting your answer for good and all. But he'd got his dander up—said your father had broke his word with him and he wouldn't be turned out like a dog, and so he's off all over the world, I expect, says he won't go home for two or years. I feel powerful bad about him; I can't bear to give this matter up so. But, my dear young lady, I will run no risks talking to you so long: you'll find a communication from your everlastin' admirer and respectful friend, Ezekiel Purson, done up in that—package of saponacous compound, madam. Much obliged to you, I'm sure. May you remain forever as young and blooming as you are at present, which

you'll be sure to do if you use my wonderful freckle-annihilat-
or, beauty-preserver, rose-cream, fragrant-foam soap.   Hope
you'll speak a good word for me to the delicate and fastidious
fair sect of your acquaintance ;" and with a wave of his hand
the talkative vender of fancy toilette articles picked up his
basket and strode away.

Edith signaled to the coachman to drive on, while she
leaned back in the carriage, of which she chanced to be the
solitary occupant, and searched the highly-scented package of
soap for the epistle spoken of.   She found it—a sheet of pink
paper, gilt-edged, very elaborately folded in a three-cornered
style, which reminded her of dairy-maids' valentines.   The
writing was of a piece with the folding—an elaborate hand,
full of stiff flourishes, and ornamented with plenty of what the
writer was wont to designate as quirlicues.

It is a curious fact that many people, whose stream of talk
will flow like an unchecked torrent, when they are called
upon to express themselves with the pen instead of the tongue,
experience a restraint which they can not overcome, and this
epistle of the loquacious Yankee began with great solemnity :

"WORTHY MISS :—I take my pen in hand to inform you
that it will be doubtful if you ever receive this, but you will
if there's wit enough in the head of Ezekiel Purson to git it to
you, which he's bound to do just as sure as you're alive.   It
may come by post, which I don't think it will, as there are
persons, or, to be more pertickeler, a person in your own home
who is like a snake in the grass—a powerful purty snake too,
with eyes like diamonds of the first water, and such person
might meddle with things sent by post, which would be nuthin' new for her.   As the Irishman said, if you never get it,
you'll know the reason why.   But, as I have matters of great
importance to communicate, you'll excuse the liberty I've
taken for old acquaintance sake, of writing to you, Miss Edith.
I am sure you do not know the fact with regard to my
nephew and his clearing out of London without an interview
with you.   Some one in your house, which *I* think was the
snake in question, but which *he* thinks was your father break-
ing his word with him, which I know Mr. Lancaster well
enough to think he wouldn't do, wouldn't allow the servants

to admit him, but sent a message, which is the worst of it, by the impudent footman, requesting he wouldn't call again, as *none* of the family wished to keep up an acquaintance which they regretted. You know my nephew well enough that he wouldn't put up with insult from the Prince of Wales himself, which that perlite young man would never give—and so he was off like a bullet out of a gun when fire tetched the powder. I seen him about an hour after; his face was as white as chalk and his eyes like coals, and so he's gone to Greece and Italy and other places, to try and forget his disappintment. I told him what you said when you was on the lawn at your father's country-house, but it didn't do much good then; perhaps when he gets cammer it'll come to mind and bring him round. And now I ask your everlasting pardon, which your kind disposition will grant, but I knew you was onaware of **fax**, and I set too much store by my boy as I call him, to see him going on so without trying to bring things about right, which will take a great while now, sence he's off so fer, but maybe you might write a letter to Italy or Jerusalem, and tell him the truth. *I* don't believe your engaged to that earl's son, though everybody else does. If you are it can't be helped, and you won't be much to blame, with such foolish parents and a hot-headed lover, who wouldn't put on a ragged coat, as *I* have, and tote around a basket of *re*-markable soap for the sake of getting word to the young lady he likes, and will always do if he don't throw himself into the crater of Vesuvius to get red of his troubles. If you are so condescending as to reply to this, you can drop a line in the penny-post to No. 30 Highflyer street, or if you hear a voice resembling the melodious aksents of Ezekiel Purson, crying out the wonderful virtues of his Freckle Exterminator, you can throw it out the winder, and he'll pick it up and no mistake. With sentiments of profound respect,

"Your everlasting friend and well-wisher,

"Ezekiel Purson."

Edith had time to read this epistle but once during the short ride to her place of destination; but two or three hours later she sat with it in her chamber, pondering over it in the twilight. Margaret wished to light the gas, but her mistress forbade her—the flickering glow of the grate was preferred by her—and she sat long, long, gazing into the fire, forgetful of her surroundings.

"Your mother desires your presence in the drawing-room, mademoiselle. There is company which inquired especially for you,"—with a meaning tone.

Reluctantly Edith arose. She knew that Arthur Beverly was coming that evening for a decisive answer to the suit which he had renewed. She knew it, for her mother had told her so. The assurances of the young lady's parents that they should never consent to her marriage with the American suitor, that he had been dismissed and had departed from the country, and that she was already forgetting him, that he, Arthur, had their full consent and approval and their warmest wishes for his success, had induced him to renew his attempt to win her love.

That morning, up to the hour she entered her carriage for the drive, Edith had resolved to accept him. She was moved by the sincerity of his affection, and she could not be insensible to the thousand graces of manner, mind, person, and position which distinguished him. She did not love him—but that was not much, since she could never marry the man she did love—she admired and respected him—should she make him as unhappy as she was herself by refusing him? Thus foolishly she had reasoned, like many another girl before her; the influence of her parents had also been powerful, and she had elated Mrs. Lancaster greatly by the signs she had given of yielding.

Now her mind suffered a sudden revolution. She was homesick. Every thing about her seemed alien and forlorn. She longed to lay her throbbing temples upon Mrs. Potter's motherly and honest breast—*there* she should meet with no deception—but only love and sympathy the tenderest. Of her step-mother, although often fascinated and won by her, she had long had doubts; she had felt as if ready affection did not prompt her actions. Now she felt as if she had been bitterly wronged by both father and mother—she did not know what Uncle Zekel had shrewdly suspected, that it was the mother who had committed all the falsehood and duplicity—that *she* had sent the message, in her husband's name, which had aroused the fiery pride of Amos. For Mr. Lancaster, as we have said before, was incapable of this rudeness. He would have received the young man courteously, kept his long appointment with him, and given him personally his objections, if he had received the card which fell by chance into his wife's hands. This woman, whom her husband still honored and confided in, despite of the bitter lesson he had learned of her powers of deception, was fated to be a thwarting genius to Edith—first, keeping her out of her home and birthright, then, after she had grown up in another, and was bound fast by clinging ties to those from whom she was torn, interfering again in the plans of her life, plotting to keep her as cunningly as she had once plotted to withhold her.

Feeling herself thus wronged, and knowing not in whom to confide—that her heart would burst with its swelling tide of grief, if she could not seek sympathy—wearied of the gayety and splendor so unsatisfactory to her, since it was so cold and false, Edith grew suddenly homesick. Not that she had not yearned often and deeply after her quiet home on that far and beautiful Western prairie; but that she now was actually feverish and ill with the intensity of her longing for her old home.

Slowly she descended to the drawing-room. If Arthur hoped the flush in her cheek was one of timidity and pleasure, he was mistaken. She was sorry for him; but she had made a resolution, as important as it was sudden. If her delicate, susceptible will had been changed to steel, she could hardly have been more firm. Her mother saw something inexplicable in her face, and troubled herself at trying to decipher it. She sang and played for Arthur when he asked her; she remarked, without confusion, the tact with which they were gradually left to themselves, to give him an opportunity of speaking to her; and when he was about to beseech her final decision in his favor, she anticipated him, saying to him quietly:

"Wait one week, Arthur. Do not say any thing to-night. Wait one week and you will receive an unequivocal answer."

"But, Edith, I have already—"

"I know, but you *must* wait."

So he went away, secretly fretting and chafing against that low-spoken "*must;*" and her step-mother was obliged to retire without knowing how matters had ended; for Edith went, immediately to her room, locked herself in, and wrote the following letter:

"Mr. Ezekiel Purson:—My dear friend. Perhaps you will think me a foolish and imprudent girl. If you do, you will tell me so plainly. But oh, I am so homesick! It seems to me as if I shall *die* if I can not see my dear old home again —if I can't throw my arms about Mrs. Potter's neck, and hear Mr. Potter say, 'How d'ye do? how d'ye do?' so glad to see me. Do you think they will really welcome me as a child? I feel as if Mrs. Potter was more my mother—as if I were more truly bound to her, by love and gratitude, than I am to this other mother. *I want to return to her.* I only promised my father to remain with him a year. I have more than fulfilled my promise, and he has broken his. I am of age, and can do as I think right. Nevertheless, I know that, if my parents were aware of my intentions, they could and would prevent my going; and for this reason it is I appeal to you. Are you going to America soon? If you are, could you be troubled with the care of an 'unprotected female?' Would you buy my passage-ticket, give me all necessary information, and help me safely on to a steamer, if you are *not* going? For, I assure you, my friend, I have *made up my mind* to go. Earthquakes can not shake my resolution. And now, my dear, good Uncle Zekel, do you think there can be any indelicacy in my going to Amos's home? You say he will not return for two or three years. Long before that I can get into some situation where I will be independent—perhaps that of a teacher of music or governess. What I want now is, to see my friends; to breathe the air of the prairies when sweet with the roses and strawberries of the coming spring; to drink out of the spring from a gourd-shell, as I used to do when a little child; to ride old Brownie; to greet the old cottage home; to be a little girl again. *They do not love me here.* My father loves me, to be sure, and I shall be sorry if my desertion grieves him; but his affection for me must be selfish, after all, or he would not thwart all the dearest wishes of my heart. I know you are truthful, and would not give

any advice that would injure the woman whom Amos once
loved. I trust you entirely. But go to America I shall,
whether you advise it or not! ("The way folks usually act
upon advice," remarked Uncle 'Zekiel, when he read it). I
want your help and knowledge as to ways and means. I
have always had a surplus of pocket-money, since I came to
London, and find I have enough laid up to pay all probable
expenses, without selling any of the costly trinkets which have
been given me. I suppose my step-mother will not regret my
leaving every thing to my half-brother, who is a fine, lovable
boy—and, if you refuse to assist me, I shall make him a con-
fidant. He will think it fine fun to assist at a runaway. I
shouldn't wonder if he should want to go with me, just for
the novelty, and come back after he'd grown tired of it. Now,
please tell me if you think it would be improper for me to
visit Amos's mother—when she is just the same to me as my
own mother? I shall be on the constant watch for an answer
to this.

    " Yours, in expectancy and hope,

                                    "E. L.'

This epistle she addressed to No. 30 Highflyer street, resolved
not to await the chances of hearing the melodious accents of
Mr. Purson crying out his Freckle Exterminator beneath her
window. It was safely received by him at the comfortable inn
at which he was putting up; for Mr. Purson was not living in
the style of a soap-vendor; but paid roundly, like all true Americans, for the best of every thing.

    "Je—hosophat! ain't she a trump! a budy would think she
was a Vermont girl, from the pluck she shows. 'Troubled
with the care of an unprotected female,'—I rather guess that's
a business 'Zekiel Purson is exactly fitted for. Selling patent-
rights comes natural, but takin' care of the fair sect comes
more so! Afraid it's unproper for her to go to Amos's mother—
the modest little critter. Je—whillikins! but wouldn't it make
Amos's heart bounce to read this letter, received by his ever-
fortunate Uncle 'Zekiel! I wish I knew where that boy was
—I'd send it to him; but Iterly ain't a *very* partickeler super-
scription, nor Greece, and it might get lost. Whew! ain't I
in luck, bearing the purtiest girl in the world clear across the
Atlantic ocean! I guess all the bisness I have on hand won't

pervent.   A man that owns a hundred thousand dollars in a
lead-mine, and twenty good-paying patent-rights, needn't confine himself to peddlin' soap when the object he had in view
is gained.   Let me see.   There's a first-class steamer sails
from Liverpool a week from yesterday.   Jest the thing!
We'll go in good style.   Don't catch Ezekiel Purson running
away at his time of life with a purty girl, 'less he does it up
brown.   Je—rusalem! but won't it be an elopement in high
life, though!   Edith, daughter of the wealthy commoner,
Edwin Lancaster, eloping with 'Zekiel Purson, Lord High-
Peddler of Patent-Rights, and Speculator in General.   Wall—
wall! let me set my wits to work to see how I'll get her away
from those folks, safe into the steamer, 'fore they're after us
and bring her back.   Them telegraphs are ugly things for
people that have sheriffs after 'em, or indignant parients.   We
might get stopped jest as we was stepping into the vessel in
high style.   Come to think, I reckon I'd better take her to
France, and get a nice packet-ship.   She can do all the jab-
bering in that confounded foreign tongue, and we'll git along
as slick as grease.

"Sho! I can't app'int any conference with her, for she
can't get out alone very well, unless it's jest for a walk in the
park—that's the idea.   I'll write to her to walk out to-morrow
morning on the square, and I'll have my plans all laid by that
time.   Je—upiter! but I wish Amos could see that letter.
I'll jest du it up and direct it to Rome, Iterly, and let it take
its chance.   If he gets it, he'll be home as fast as steam can
bring him.   Teach school! oh, ho! I think I see 'Zekiel Purson a-letting her, with a hundred thousand dollars in the lead-
mines.   She shall have that cottage and farm I bought of
James Pipkin, and be heir to half my property, and Amos to
t'other half, whether they ever get married or not—for which
I pray with all my heart.   'Zekiel Purson is just in his element when he's hatching out a secret plan—he's got as much
of a faculty for contrivin' things as the old woman had that
was cuttin' and contrivin' all day to get a night-cap out of a
sheet.   Oh, my! let me get my pen and ink and paper, and
keep this ball a-rolling."

Mr. Purson was in a great state of exhilaration; an hour
later, his strong, nasal tones were ringing the virtues of his

soap upon the aristocratic air of Portman square. When Edith heard him, in the distance, she threw on her cloak and bonnet and went out for a few moments' walk in the fresh air, coming in with such rosy cheeks that her father recommended her to go out more frequently. In obedience to this suggestion, she went out the following morning for a promenade in the safe precincts of the square; and two mornings after that she went out and came back no more.

They found a note in her room, after searching her escritoir, addressed to her father, saying :

"DEAR FATHER :—I regret leaving you; but I am homesick—I *must* go home. Do not suffer any alarm about me. I shall be safe under the escort of Mr. Purson, who, I am sure, is as honorable as he is kind. I have no other company, and am going to visit Mrs. Potter.

"Your affectionate daughter,

"EDITH."

CHAPTER XI.

"IT's a-blowing terribly, Miss Edith, terribly. I think it's best to tell you, so you can be up and dressed and ready for the wust. The captain thinks we're nigh onto the rocks, and if we get on *them* we're lost, sure as preachin'."

"Won't you let me go up on deck, Uncle 'Zekiel?"

"Mercy no! you'd be blown or washed overboard in less'n five minits."

"I'd rather be washed into the sea than drowned in a little hole like this," pleaded Edith, looking about her narrow state-room.

"The other three ladies are in the cabin, as white as ghosts. You'd better go out and keep 'em company. O Lord, Miss Edith, I'm everlastin' sorry I took you away from your father. You'd been a sleepin' safe and sound in your silk coverlids there, instid of being pitched about by this infernal tempest."

"Don't reproach yourself, Uncle 'Zekiel. It was I who took myself away. If I did wrong, I hope to be forgiven for it—it seemed to me that I was doing right. I'm not so *very* much afraid to die—are you?" and she looked at him wistfully.

"Why, as to that, my dear, if I must die, I trust to meet death like a man; but I'll fight it like a man, too, be sure of that. I've got you into this mess, and if there's any thing to be done to get you out of it, I'll do it. Make yourself easy that I'll go first, if we have to go."

"There! I've got my shawl on and my hood. Let me go out on deck with you; I'd rather be where you are than anywhere else."

"And you shall be. I shan't leave you. But you'd perish of cold and the salt spray freezing on you, almost, if you'd go out. Don't go till you *have* to—time enough then. See here my dear; here's a patent life-preserver—it seems like an uncommon good kind; I got two before we sailed; I'm going to fasten this one around you, and the other I'm going to give to that sickly lady with the little babe."

" What are you going to do ?"

"Me? If the wust comes to the wust, I'll stick to a board. I reckon. There's plenty of life-preservers on board, but they ain't good for much. But, Lord, the rocks and the bitter wind will soon put an end to us, if we once get on 'em."

" Are there life-boats ?"

" Yes ! but it's a question if they could live in this sea."

They went out into the little cabin of the packet-ship where her few passengers were huddled together silent, with strained nerves, listening to the booming of the waves, the shrieking of the wind, the creaking of the timbers. Uncle 'Zekiel fastened the life-preserver on the delicate woman with the infant, who had no protector on board, and who thanked him with a look. A wolfish man, a German, appeared as if he would like to tear it from her, if he dared.

Upon a table in the cabin were the remains of the captain's supper—some slices of corned beef and a plate of sea-biscuit, with pickles and cheese. Edith staggered up to the table and began putting them in the pocket and bosom of her dress—she was thinking of starvation at sea, in an open boat, if they should have to take to the boats.

"Here is a bottle of the captain's wine—I'll take it for your baby, ma'am," said Ezekiel, comprehending what Edith was about, and speaking to the invalid—and he put the pint bottle in his pocket.

At that moment the vessel pitched fearfully and went down—down, with a sliding motion which made each one hold their breath ; and, when they drew it again, it was with a scream, for there was an awful shock—the ship had struck a rock !

" We're all lost !" cried the captain, appearing at the door. " The water is rushing in in torrents—there's nothing can keep it down. I would to God that it at least was daylight but it's two hours to sunrise yet."

Even as he spoke, water appeared in the cabin. The passengers joined the crew on the deck ; the darkness itself

was horrible, the lamps casting a faint glimmer upon the deck
through the spray which dimmed them.

"The boats will swamp, if we lower them," said the captain.
"Let us remain upon the ship as long as possible."

The vessel seemed to have settled as much as she was going
to—the hurricane deck was above the water, though the waves
occasionally dashed over it. But few provisions could be
got out, as they were so suddenly submerged; what there
were, were placed in the two boats, which were ready to lower
if opportunity offered.

The women were secured with ropes from being washed
overboard; Ezekiel obtained a piece of the canvas with which
he partially defended them from the bitter wind and spray.
So the dreary minutes went by like ages, until the gray dawn
lightened and betrayed to them more fully their appalling
situation. Yet they felt that certainty was worse than suspense.
There was no land in sight, as the captain knew. They had
been out four days, but for the last thirty-six hours had been
blown back by the gale, losing, instead of making progress,
and the rocks they were now upon were an ugly ledge which
lay a couple of hundred miles from the southern shore of
France.

The storm had been abating for some time, and the wind
no longer blew violently, though the waves yet rolled fearfully
high.

"It is better than if there was a rock-bound coast behind
us, to be driven upon in case we are washed off," said the
captain. "The vessel won't hold together fifteen minutes more,
I don't believe. My lads, lower the boats, and put the women
in first."

This difficult and dangerous work was now attempted. The
sick lady was lowered first, while Mr. Purson held her child,
and then swung into the boat to receive it, lest it should be
dashed to death against the vessel's side. Then Edith and the
other two women were lowered into his arms. There was
room for all in the two boats, if they could only keep them
from swamping; and they had oars to steer by. The moment
the first boat had received its complement, it pulled away
through the frightful sea which threatened to engulf it every
instant. The ship was already breaking up, and the second

boat cleared her just in time to escape the swirl in which she finally disappeared.

"It is but two hundred miles to land, if we can keep our boats from the rocks," and the captain plied an oar with the rest.

An hour later, they felt comparatively safe. They bailed the water out which ran in occasionally; the sun shone out, and the waves were running themselves out. But the people were wet and shivering, dreadfully cold and fatigued, and, after a while, hungry. There was a water-cask in their boat; but, by some strange fatality, the provisions were all in the other boat. However, this would not be so bad, for the boats were bound to keep together.

"The women will all perish, they're such delicate critters, before we make land," said Mr. Purson.

He took off his overcoat and wrapped it about the purple infant, while Edith soaked a piece of biscuit with the port-wine and fed it.

"May I be drawn and quartered if ever I attempt to run away with a purty girl again," muttered Uncle Zekiel, looking dolefully at Edith's pallid face, shining out of its clinging hair; but she forced a smile, shaking her head archly even then.

That night the boats, somehow, in the black darkness, drifted apart; and in the morning there was nothing to eat. They had no light, and even the sailors' guiding-star was obscured, so that it was useless to ply the oars, and they had made no progress during the night.

Edith divided her little store of sea-biscuit, one to each of the company, and two to the baby; and Ezekiel put his away without eating it.

A second time the night came down upon them—a second time the dawn brightened, this time, indeed, with unspeakable brightness.

"A sail! a sail!"

"O God, grant that they see us!" prayed the mother of the child.

"Ah, yes! they are standing toward us!"

A glow pervaded every heart, which warmed and fed them by anticipation.

The ship which laid by for them was a vessel sailing from

Genoa for New York—an American vessel at that, with several lady passengers.

"Je—whillikins! but we're in luck!" cried Mr. Purson, immediately recovering from every fatigue, when he read the name of the vessel.

Soon the shipwrecked mariners were safely on board.

"We picked up the rest of your crew six hours ago, and were on the look-out for you," said one captain to another. Then, indeed, there were hearty congratulations.

"Je—hosophat!" cried Uncle Ezekiel, bounding suddenly forward and catching some one by the coat-collar.

Edith looked and beheld—Amos! homeward bound.

"What on airth! snakes and punkins! Well, I must say, this is about the greatest arrangement—there! there! look to that critter! I do believe she's goin' to faint away, and no wonder. Catch her, Amos! I shan't tech her! I've had trouble enough with her. The next time your uncle attempts to run away with a purty girl may we have a wuss time than we've had now."

Amos bore Edith down to the cabin, where kind-hearted ladies cared for her. While these were giving her restoratives smoothing out her tangled hair, and arraying her in fresh garments contributed from their own wardrobes, Uncle Ezekiel was expatiating upon the "fax of the case," to Amos—repentant, self-reproaching, yet eager, exultant Amos.

That voyage to New York was surely a trip to Paradise; the sails were silver, the cordage golden, the breezes blown from fairy-land; the captain and crew were heroes, romantic in tarpaulin; the blue ocean recovered its charms and lost its terrors—for the rich sunshine of two happy hearts gilded every thing.

"Since I've got this highly-important business off my hands, I'll have to 'tend to my patents a little more to pass away the time. To be sure, I've lost all my models, etc., but I can kind of explain things, and perhaps induce some of these gentlemen to take an interest, when we arrive in port. Tell you what it is, Amos, I wished I'd a left her to home, to her proud parents and that nice young man, when the storm came up, and the wind blew them tremendous big guns. But it's turned out jest as it oughter, and I'll never doubt Providence again. She hain't a penny left—even the gownd she's got on is borrowed. But I'll give her a setting-out, my boy, plenty good enough for the place she's goin' to live in."

So the ship came safely to port, and the lovers landed upon their native shore. It was the day of her arrival, as Mr. Ezekiel Purson was returning to the vessel for some of Amos's "traps," that he espied, fidgeting along the dock, the queer, nice little figure of his old friend and mortal enemy, James Pipkin.

"Hello! you don't say so! Where have you turned up from, Mr. Pipkin? *Glad* to see you. How *do* you do? How's your folks?" and he held out his huge hand in the most innocent manner.

"Where's my young lady? answer me that, this instant. Where's Miss Edith?" almost screamed James, ignoring the obtrusive hand.

"Why! ain't she to home?" queried Ezekiel, with the utmost *sang froid.*

"You know she isn't—you know you stole her away like a thief in the night from her own father, and from being married to the best young gentleman in Hingland."

" I did, did I ?"

" You know you did !" said James, shaking with wrath.

" You don't s'pose I could give the mitten to a nice young girl like that, when she asked me, out-and-out, to run away with her ?"

" *She!* Miss Edith, forsooth ! tell me where she is, this instant."

"I don't know jest where she is this instant."

"Oh, come now, no fooling—where is she ?"

" Supposing I don't want to tell—then what ?"

" Then—then, I'll—I'll—" and James shrunk back from the laughing malice in the eye of the tall Vermonter, "have you arrested for abduction."

" Sho ! Mr. Pipkin, I wouldn't, if I was in your place."

" Well—my master will."

" Where is your master?"

" He's in the city, on the look-out for you. He got the start of you—you—rascally Yankee you !"

" Wall, just tell him, with my complements, that the ship

his darter sailed in was shipwrecked, and went down in less'n no time."

"Are you in earnest ?" asked James, his jaw falling, and staring at his adversary with a distressed look.

"Never more so. *I* only escaped by the skin of my teeth."

"O Lord ! and what became of *her ?*"

"She drifted off in an open boat, without any provisions."

' Oh—oh—oh ! Lord 'ave mercy !"

"He *did* have mercy."

"He did—how ? Do you know any thing more what became of my blessed young lady—my own child, as it were ?"

"She was picked up by a homeward-bound vessel,—this very one here—"

"The Lord be praised !"

"And on that vessel, by the luckiest chance, was our young friend, Amos Potter, to whose care I committed her."

"Oh ! blast it !"

"I've just come from seein' 'em married, by a regler orthodox minister, that done the ceremony up brown."

"Fire and fury !"

"Fact ! fact, my friend. They'll start on their bridal-tower to-morrow, I expect. Goin' West. So, you see, you're a *leetle* too late. Give my best respects to Mr. Lancaster, and tell him his darter's well settled in life, and hopes he'll come and see her when she's set up in housekeepin'. What's bred in the bone will come out in the flesh. Jest put him in mind of a certain little trip he took himself, in his young days, and advise him not to bother the young folks."

"Where is Miss Edith stopping ?"

"Mrs. Potter, I beg your parding."

"Mrs. Potter, then. At what hotel are they stopping ?"

"Oh, you get eout ! Don't s'pose I'm goin' to tell you, now. I shall advise 'em not to stop at any, but make tracks as fast as possible."

"If they be really married, they better see the father. Maybe he'll relent enough to give his daughter a little something to begin in the world with."

"*I* shall 'tend to that matter, Mr. Pipkin. She'll have a pile of rocks, before many years, sure as my name is 'Zekiel Purson. She can live without any charity bestowed by condescending relatives, and it's *my* opinion that Amos Potter would kick every darned dollar out of doors that her friends would have the impudence to toss to her. There! chaw that!"

"I'd like to see her and bid her good-by,—she's dear to me as a child of my own," whimpered Mr. Pipkin.

"Oh, yes! she's so dear to you and all the rest of 'em, you'd ruther break her heart, and shet her up like a squirrel in a cage, where she'd pine away and die for the blessed woods and perraries, than let her have her will and marry the finest youngster that ever grew up,—I won't except your earl's son, though he was a mighty fine chap—but in the real grit, after all, he couldn't hold a candle to Amos, and if he could, *she* didn't fancy him, and that's the main pint. Je-whillikins! .here comes the old chap himself, looking as glum as a basket of chips. Now you'll see these butes of mine do good service. Good-by, Mr. Pipkin,"—and taking to his heels, Mr. Purson strode away in a long trot that would have distanced any man's best running.

CHAPTER XII

MRS. POTTER was busy in her kitchen. Though she had been prospered beyond her expectations, and was abundantly able to keep "help," she still, like a good old-fashioned house-keeper, preferred to do her own work in her own way. It "worried her dreadfully" to see flaunting Irish girls break-ing up her crockery, battering her bright tin-ware, spilling grease on her white floor, and smashing things generally. She had only herself and Peter to do for when the boys were away, and she could not accustom herself to sit idle in the parlor while things were going to destruction in the kitchen; so she performed all her household avocations, and lived in a state of neatness, peace, and comfort indescribable.

On this particular morning she was busying herself as much to drive away thought as because there was any thing to do.

The butter was churned, worked over, made into pats and put away; there was no extra work of any kind on hand.

"I don't know what to get for Peter's dinner," she mused; "it's so hard getting any thing new at this season of the year."

The door stood wide open for the first time that spring. It was yet in the "stormy March," but no day could be imagined more beautiful. A warm wind, sweet with the tint of coming violets, was blown about the world; the sky had that tender tint of blue which it wears at no other time, and light white clouds drifted in dreamy slowness through mid-air; in the little flower-beds which came up to the flags, with which the space immediately before the door was paved, the crocuses and hyacinths were beginning to unfold their purple and white, while one yellow daffodil had opened its eyes and was smiling at them.

The door stood wide open, and if the earth was thrilled with an awakening consciousness of beauty without, the homely kitchen too had a charm of its own. The cotton-wood floor was white and spotless; the tin pans for the milking, bright as hot water and soap could make them, hung in shining rows against one side of the wall; every utensil was clean and in its place, while the delicious aroma of browning coffee sent out a rival challenge to the south wind.

"I'm sure I don't know what to get;" and Mrs. Potter sat down in a splint-bottom chair, and smoothing down her apron, looked out of doors—there was a quiver about her mouth, and tears in her eyes, which the difficulty about dinner had certainly not brought there. "-It's the wust season of the year for cookin'. The punkins and apples are gone, so there's nothing for pies—and nobody likes dried-apples—leastwise Peter don't. The spring chickens ain't big enough to cook, and the last year's are too old; the vegetables have give out mostly. Dear! dear! well, there's plenty of fresh eggs and cream, and I'll cook up somethin'. I'll have ham and eggs, mashed potatoes, parsnips stewed in cream—and, come to think, I do believe the sparrowgrass is large enough to cut—sparrowgrass on toast—and I'll jest bake a nice, rich, turnover short-cake, split it open, butter it, and spread it with strawberry jam—short-cake pie is one of Peter's favorites—he'll make out, he'll make out;" and having settled the dinner question, she sighed and sat looking mournfully at the pretty crocuses.

The reason of the good lady's disquiet was a letter received from Amos, the previous evening, in which he had told his parents enough of the treatment he had received in London to make them understand that he was bitterly angry and disappointed; that he had forsworn his hopes of Edith; that he was unspeakably wretched—and he added his resolve to cure his heart-soreness by travel in distant lands, and that they need not expect to see him for a couple of years. Grief for the disappointment of her darling, a mother's resentment of the causes of his trouble, and loneliness at the prospect of his long absence, all conspired to fill the slow fountains of her tears, until at last they trickled over.

"Dear me! it seems no longer ago than yesterday since they was little bits of things, playing about the floor. Every thing comes back to me so plain to-day. It was just such a day as this old Pipkin took such a scare with the Injins, seventeen years ago. Laws! I've laughed till the tears run down many and many a time, when I thought about his hiding under the bed with his baby. What a sweet little baby she was! the loveliest, the happiest little critter, and she was always jist as sweet and pleasant. If she's spiled they've spiled her; but it don't seem to me as if any thing could really change Edith Lancaster. I'm sure that silly old James of her's tried hard enough. Well, well, I couldn't help likin' him, with all his oddity, he was so devoted to that child. He'd have cut off his head to please her if she'd asked him. They say mothers is hard to please in their sons' wives, but if Amos had married *her* I'd have been content. Poor boy! poor boy! nobody but *me* knows how his heart was sot on her. He hain't rested since she went away. And now—

"There's the old log-house down to the end of the garden where she used to frolic when she was a little girl. Peter wouldn't have it tore down, and now it's jist run over with rose-vines and morning-glories; and I've sometimes thought maybe *their* children would use it for a play-house. Heigho!

"La! if Peter should see I'd been a-crying it would make him feel all down, and spile his appetite. I might as well be busy about somethin'. Them eggs look so nice I believe I'll

bake some cake.   Amos used to like my seed-cakes;"—and
Mrs. Potter bustled about, getting the necessary ingredients
and dishes.   There was something cheerful in the click of the
egg-beater, and the sight of the great platter of foamy eggs, in
the "handsome" way in which the compound came together,
and afterward rose to the highest pitch of lightness, and
acquired just the proper shade of brown in the oven.

There was something very cheerful in the way the sunshine
lay upon the white floor, and the birds came to pick up
crumbs from the yard; and insensibly, as she worked away,
the spirits of Mrs. Potter rose, like her cake.

"Dan'l always said Amos would never get that girl, and I
expect he'll crow over his good guessing when he hears the
news.   Dan'l never was as ambitious for learnin' and smart
society as Amos, and I begin to think his plain common
sense is goin' to make him the happiest of the two.   He's
getting monstrous rich out of those lead mines.   The last time
he was to home he said he'd be a millionaire some day.   But I'd
ruther he wouldn't give himself up to it quite so much.   I
must get Peter to write him a letter to-night.   I really wish
he'd get married and settle down close by,—it's hard to be
childless, as it were, now that we're growing old.   This cake
is beautiful—fit for a bride, I declare!" and she lifted it from
the oven and sat it down upon the table—"it's riz up even all
over.   I've seen many a bride-cake that wasn't as handsome."

She heard a step at the door, and a shadow fell athwart
the sunshine upon the floor.

"You home a-ready, Peter?" she inquired, without looking
around; "I haven't begun dinner yet.   It's only 'leven
o'clock."

A light step flitted over the threshold, a pair of soft arms
were thrown about her neck, and before she knew at all how
it came about, Edith lay upon her bosom, laughing and crying.

"Dear mother, here I am—*home* at last!"

"And you're willin' to call this home, are you?" queried
Mrs. Potter.

"But it *is* my home, and you are *my* mother," continued
Edith, with a blush.   "Tell her all about it, Amos."

And then Amos stepped out from his concealment behind
the door, and after kissing his mother, introduced her to his

wife, Mrs. Amos Potter. And there were both smiles and tears.

"Sho! ain't you goin' to let the fellow that took the most conspicuous part in bringing about this state of things take a part in these interestin' proceedings?"—and Uncle Zekie. appeared from the front parlor, where he'd been standing, taking observations, having accompanied the young people on their "bridal tower," and being eager to take part in the "surprise party."

To the graphic powers of Mr. Purson was left the delightful task of narrating all the whys and wherefores of this sudden change He told the story to Mellissy, while she listened, forgetful of dinner. And the other two actors laughed secretly at that fearful faculty of exaggeration which betrayed itself in his exciting narrative. He dwelt with thrilling emphasis upon the storm at sea—(it was from this time observable that with every repetition of the tale its horrors increased, until a year later it had grown to such frightful proportions that no other shipwreck ever compared with it— the waves rising five hundred feet, the wind cutting up things generally like a sharp knife, taking all the hair out of the heads of those who didn't protect themselves by wrapping them in canvas, the ship going to pieces in five minutes, and the company drifting about without food or water for fifteen days,—and if Mr. Purson should be spared to tell the story to his nephew's little ones, there's no saying to what still more stupendous height it may aspire)—and with great gusto upon his interview with James upon the wharf, and how neatly they evaded pursuit, taking the first train out of the city, and spending the first night after the wedding "riding on the rail!"

"I forget there was such a thing as dinner to be got," ejaculated Mrs. Potter, when she had heard all, "and you must be right-down hungry, riding so far since breakfast. "Here, Zekiel, make yourself useful and slice the ham while I'm settin' the table."

"Your most obedient, marm," said Mr. Purson, taking up the knife with one of his flourishes; "it's my mission to be useful, 'specially to the fair sect. How many slices?"

"Oh, jist as many as you think we'll eat. It's as nice as

chicken, that ham is; we fed the pork ourselves, on corn, and Peter cured it. It's smoked with corn-cobs."

"There's one for Peter, and one for Mellissy, and two for Amos, and this little bit of a one for the bride, and one—two—three—four for your humble servant! Fact is, ever sence I come so nigh being starved in that boat at sea, I've had an uncommon appetite. Have to make up for lost time. You know I used to be a small eater—never *used* to eat but three slices of ham and five or six fried eggs—but now I think I'm equal to as many as eight. Had a nasty breakfast at the railroad station, and I'm powerful hungry. Allow eight eggs for me, Mellissy."

"Eggs are plenty since this warm spell," replied the housewife, good-naturedly. "I shan't stint you, Zekiel. Now what on airth do you s'pose put it into my head to bake this cake this mornin'? Me and Peter seldom eat cake; and when I'd made it, and got it all done, I was jist sayin' to myself t'was handsome enough for a bride. Wasn't that curious?"

"Rather a singular coincidence—remarkable, in fact, and can't be accounted for on any principle less it's that of magnetism and pursentiment combined—a science I am very familiar with. Hide behind the door, sis, there comes Potter."

As the farmer came to his kitchen door the hand of his son reached out and grasped his, and white arms were about his neck, and a pair of lips on his cheek—a flood of sunshine that lightened instantaneously the gloom which had oppressed him all day.

"So I've got a daughter at last, have I, Mellissy?" he asked, with a smile, as they all gathered about the homely, happy board; "you've always promised me one, though I'd about given up hopes."

"You may go to work and make as much more of that cake as you're a mind to," said Uncle Zekiel, when he had demolished an undue share of the dinner. "I'm bound to have the greatest infair this country ever saw. I'll pay the fiddler myself. I want Daniel sent for, and everybody within ten miles invited. I'm great on frolics, you know, and I think the occasion warrants the tallest kind of one."

"I'm agreed, with all my heart," said Mr. Potter.

So Uncle Zekiel set himself to work to get up the infair.

Word was sent by special messenger to Daniel, and it was calculated that he could arrive the third evening from this, and the invitations were given out accordingly.

Edith had to have a dress made for the occasion, as the brown stuff in which she had actually been married was hardly suitable. The evening came, fair and prosperous; the joyous company assembled, and amidst them was Daniel, a tall and business-looking young man, who remarked to his brother, with one regretful look into the face of the adorable bride—

"You always were too quick for me, Amos. I'd have tried my fortunes in that direction long ago, but I knew you'd cut me out."

It would have done anybody's heart good to have seen the faces of the father and mother that evening—so shining with inward delight, content, and pride. For once in his life Uncle Zekiel laid aside all business, and did not try to strike up a single bargain; he mingled no mention of patent-rights with his humor. Once indeed he forgot himself in a distant allusion: having danced the "Virginny reel" with a red-cheeked girl, and kept it up for an incredible length of time, he remarked that "when he was dancin' the Virginny reel he was like one of his eight-day clocks, he never knew when to run down—a few of which could still be bought at a bar—" but here he checked himself, and appeared to regret the subject.

While the festivities were at their height, there came an intrusion which might reasonably be regarded as a remarkable coincidence, if the reader's memory will go back to the cornhusking.

Again Mr. Lancaster appeared suddenly upon the scene, with James in his retinue. He had first sought and obtained a few moments' interview with Mrs. Potter, who now brought him forward and introduced him to the bride and groom, whom he congratulated in so cordial a manner as to prove that he had made a virtue of necessity, and had obtained the mastery over any unpleasant feeling he had cherished.

"I am glad to see you looking so very happy, my child and since such has been your choice, such your taste and idea of happiness, perhaps it is for the best that you have followed your own inclinations. What I regret most is, that we must of necessity be separated by so many thousands of miles. I hope that you, Amos, will not fail to bring my daughter to visit me at intervals. I am needed at home now; but I could not, being so near you, turn back across the ocean before I had seen you, Edith, and bid you farewell and God speed."

"And I couldn't go back at all," said James, coming forward through the company. "I couldn't no more live without you to tend upon, Miss Edith, than I could without the light of my eyes. I forgives everybody, even Mr. Purson, and will serve Mr. Amos Potter the same as if he were a nobleman born, if you'll only let me stay with you, Miss Edith, and wait upon you as long as I live."

"My dear old James," said the bride, with tears shining through her smile, "I knew you loved me truly. Yes, stay! I should like nothing so much."

"Shake hands, old fellow," cried Mr. Purson, coming up and seizing James' hand, "my respeck for you has riz like a pot of yeast, Mr. Pipkin—you've behaved like a man, spite of your bringin' up, and your small statue. Let by-gones be by-gones. If anybody ever offers to fight you, let me know, and I'll shake it out of him. You can count on me as your friend and defender, for Providence made you little, and you can't fight your own battles. Yes-sir-ee! I'll stick to you, Mr. Pipkin, as long as you stick to Madame Potter here. Je-whillikins! but you're a great old customer, Mr. Pipkin. Can you dance? No? I wish you could, I'd have you introduced to the nicest girl in the country. I declare, I hain't been so pleased since that time I left you on the wharf. Oh, cracky! whew! strike up there, fiddler! I can't contain myself! Me and Mr. Pipkin are a-going to dance!"—and seizing James in his powerful arms, he lifted him to the points of his toes and spun round and round with him till the little old man gasped for mercy.

"'Taint exactly etiquette," he remarked, turning, with a ludicrous bow of pretended apology, to Mr. Lancaster, "to have our hired help a-dancin' in the parlor, even on the occasion of a wedding, but you see, James, he could'nt help it, and aughter be excused."

"Oh, certainly," replied he, not knowing what else to say

"It ain't etiquette to deliver lectures upon an occasion like the present—leastwise less it's curtain-lectures, which is the privilege of the bride. But I've got a weakness for lecturing —it's broke out several times, quite unexpectedly to my friends. Once I went around speakin' on temperance—once I made a phrenological tower feelin' of fools' heads for a dollar a-piece, and telling 'em tremendous whoppers—all the young men was unappreciated geniuses, and all the young women was bilin' and bustin' over with repressed affection, &c.; all the little boys was future presidents, and all the little girls was going to grow up poetesses, &c., by which I made a good many dollars. Once I gave a course of lectures on physico-magnetism, and electro-foreknowledge, which was deservedly popular, and give me considerable eminence as a narrator and man of science. However, as I was sayin', a social frolic ain't the place for a lecture, and I've no intentions of deliverin' one —all I want to relieve my mind of is a few remarks about Love !" Here Mr. Purson took so striking an attitude, although particularly addressing Mr. Lancaster, that a group gathered about him which gradually comprised the whole assembly. "Love, sir, is a great institution. I may say it is ekil, if not superior, to the Constitution of the United States, and everybody knows that's a great institution. Do you know what makes this country so surprisingly superior to every other on the face of the globe ?—it's *love*, sir ! When young folks here fall in love, they git married. Here ain't no noblemen's sons to have the first piek of all the purty girls —proud parents don't *sell* their children, like cattle in the market, to the highest bidder—no-sir-ee ! I rather guess they don't—and if they did, the young people wouldn't put up with it, but would jine hands at the nearest minister's. Now, I know an old lady that says all she had to begin with when her and Hezekiah got married, was a dish-kittle. 'We used,' says she, 'to bile our potatoes, and turn 'em out into a cracked plate ; then we fried our pork, and then we steeped our coffee, all in the dish-kittle, and when we got through, we fed the pig in it ! Folks can do a great deal with a dish-kittle, if they've only a mind,' says the old lady. Wall, I don't exact-ly like the latter stage of the old lady's proceedings, myself— but if folks thought more of real happiness, and less of show, there'd be a great many more love-matches. A love-match !

What is there ekil to it? I pause for a reply; in the language of that gentleman and scholard,

Uncle Zekiel,
There's *nothin'* ekil.

"The very subjick transmogrifies me into a poet, and causes me to bust out into rhyme. My feelin's rise right up to the bilin' point, and bubble over in effervescent spasmodies. I become like a bottle of beer that's blowed it's cork out—whiz —fizz! The poetry runs out of my mouth and I can't stop it I'm an old bachelor, myself, which is a great pity, especially for the fair sect. I don't speak so much from experience as from observation. But if I ever *do* get noosed, which ain't unlikely, I'll go into the bonds with the girl that I like and that likes me, if she hain't even a dish-kittle to her name. Yes-sir-ee! better marry a pretty girl that you love, if she's so poor she has to go barefooted to the preacher's, than hitch horses with some woman you don't have a weakness for, if she's as rich as all Californy. And if you love your daughter as you aughter, better let her have her choice, if she *does* pick out an American without any title to his name, than compel her to have somebody she don't care a snap of her finger for. Je-whillikins, yes! decidedly! Amos is a smart young man, and I look forward to his being in the Cabinet before he's sixty, and I'm certain he'll be worth his weight in diamonds. He loves Edith, and she loves him, and they've run away and got married. Jemime! I wish 'em joy, don't you? If you'll trouble yourself to think back nineteen or twenty years maybe you'll remember a young gentleman who did the same—who run away with a Scotch preacher's darter, against the advice of his parients, for the simplest reason in the world—because he loved her. The stars are a shinin' on her grave to-night, Mr. Lancaster, but I believe that her angelic spirit looks down from heaven and rejoices in the happiness of her child—her blessin' rests upon her daughter— Amen."

CHAPTER XII.

ANOTHER MARRIAGE.

"I HAVE always said that I would never marry a man who did not offer me a heart which was mine exclusively—who did not honor me with his *first* love.   I want no battered and bruised affections which have been played with by one and another until all their freshness is gone!" and the young girl threw back her head proudly, gazing full into the eyes of her suitor.

"But this is my first *love*, Madeline."

"I have always heard that you were a lover of Edith Lancaster's."

"Well, I *did* fancy her; I even imagined I loved her. She was *my cousin*, you know, and very pretty and amiable. But I did not break my heart when she ran away to America, and I *should*, dear Madeline, if *you* should prefer another to me.   I did not know my own heart then, my own tastes, what would please me best and most enduringly—*now* I know ! I fancied her—I adore you!   When she left me, I was miserable for a week—should you refuse me I shall be unhappy forever.   You do not want this weight upon your conscience, do you, sweet Madeline?—that you have ruined my hopes, palsied my ambition, doomed me to the loneliness of a solitary life?   Surely you have magnanimity enough (for I see it in that noble countenance) to forget that I once fancied myself attached to another.   Even *then*, while that dream was still upon me, one chance glimpse of you, a stranger, unknown to me,—one chance sight of your face, haunted me with a pertinacity which would not be overcome—which led me, finally, to seek you out and throw myself at your feet.   Do not let a maiden's fanciful resolve stand between us and life-long happiness.   You love me, Madeline, do you not?—as I do you, with the love which is immortal."

"Answer the question as you please, Arthur," and her eyes sank, while, with a burning blush, she hid them on his shoulder.

This scene took place upon one of the balconies of an old castle, which stood upon a height, commanding views alike of the peaceful glens below and the towering mountains above —the castle of a Scottish earl, which had been the stronghold of the family in olden times of feudal warfare, and its home at the present day.

Arthur Beverly, in that wild tour which he had taken, the previous summer, while under the influence of Edith's rejection, was one day wandering alone amid crags, ravines, cascades, and precipices, admiring the wild grandeur of the scene, when, turning the brow of a rocky height, he had came face to face with this noble old castle, and beheld suddenly, upon the balcony, a vision of beauty so fair and serene, so proud yet so gentle, that wonder and admiration kept him gazing long upon the unexpected sight. With the fair, gold-tinted hair of her country, the exquisite complexion, she had with it a majestic form and a face full of sweetness and nobility—the pride of birth and purity combined with the gentleness of a woman's warm heart.

When Arthur went back to the cottage where he slept that night, he inquired about the castle and its occupants. When the name and rank of the owner was mentioned, he knew him, at once, by reputation, and that his father had met him frequently. He knew that if he should introduce himself to the castle he would be welcomed, and its hospitalities urged upon him; but his heart was too sore, his mind too engrossed, for him to wish to trouble himself with being agreeable in return for courtesies received.

The cottager was enthusiastic in praise of the earl's daughter —the most beautiful, the most innocent, the most benevolent angel that had ever dwelt in the castle, though it had been the home of many a peerless Scottish lady. The Lady Madeline was proud only to the forward or the arrogant; to the poor she was kind and gentle, and good to all. "If the young Lord Beverly would present himself at the castle, who knew what might come of it?" But Arthur was not then in a mood to seek adventures.

A year later, it seems he *was* in the mood. Not two months after the flight of Edith, the memory of that golden-haired daughter of Scotia began to float before him in a radiant atmosphere of romance and rose-tinged reality. The more he thought of it, the sweeter the vision grew. He was seized with a desire to repeat his Northern tour, and the autumn of that summer shone upon the scene as here related; and the family of one earl soon received proposals from the other for the arrangement of a marriage in every way proper and satisfactory.

There are two sides to every question; and the question of love is not an exception, notwithstanding the eloquent peroration of our friend, Mr. Purson, in the preceding chapters. We give a passing view of both sides, without seeking to throw our influence to either.

Edith will probably soon have the pleasure of reading, in the *Court Journal,* a full description of the magnificent wedding, the dresses of the bride, bride-maid, god-mother, and other attendants; the marriage presents, jewels, etc., which will lighten her foolish conscience, which still shrinks from the fear that it has inflicted misery upon a manly and deserving heart.

In the mean time, Edith is receiving *her* bridal presents by degrees. Uncle Zekiel has presented her with the farm and cottage in which she was born; Daniel has sent her a handsome tea-service of silver, and other articles of the same, from the proceeds of only one of his numerous shares in the Galena lead-mines, and Mr. Potter has given her money to build an elegant new mansion in place of the rustic cottage, which the check her father left with her will amply furnish.

The young married couple are living with their parents at present, but their own home, a marvel of beauty and taste, is nearly finished, and James is looking forward eagerly to the pleasure and honor of waiting upon his mistress in her own establishment. Uncle Zekiel is at present in Vermont, visiting old friends, but as soon as Edith gets to housekeeping—"Jemima! but I reckon I'll go and see how she looks at it!" he says. He has taken an interest in a new sewing-machine, which will afford him an excuse for a journey West, combining business and pleasure, according to his favorite theory.

www.ingramcontent.com/pod-product-compliance
Lightning Source LLC
Chambersburg PA
CBHW022139020726
47496CB00008B/2466